W9-AOZ-016

WITHDRAWN

THIRST

VARSHA BAJAJ

Nancy Paulsen Books

Nancy Paulsen Books
An imprint of Penguin Random House LLC, New York

First published in the United States of America by Nancy Paulsen Books,
an imprint of Penguin Random House LLC, 2022

Copyright © 2022 by Varsha Bajaj

Penguin supports copyright. Copyright fuels creativity, encourages diverse voices, promotes free
speech, and creates a vibrant culture. Thank you for buying an authorized edition of this book
and for complying with copyright laws by not reproducing, scanning, or distributing any part of it
in any form without permission. You are supporting writers and allowing Penguin to continue to
publish books for every reader.

Nancy Paulsen Books & colophon are trademarks of Penguin Random House LLC.

Visit us online at penguinrandomhouse.com

Library of Congress Cataloging-in-Publication Data
Names: Bajaj, Varsha, author.
Title: Thirst / Varsha Bajaj.
Description: New York: Nancy Paulsen Books, [2022] | Summary: "A heroic girl in
Mumbai fights for her belief that water should be for everyone"—Provided by publisher.
Identifiers: LCCN 2022000703 (print) | LCCN 2022000704 (ebook) |
ISBN 9780593354391 (hardcover) | ISBN 9780593354407 (ebook)
Subjects: LCSH: Water security—India—Mumbai—Juvenile fiction. | LCGFT: Fiction.
Classification: LCC PZ7.B1682 Tf 2022 (print) | LCC PZ7.B1682 (ebook) |
DDC [Fic]—dc23/eng/20220114
LC record available at https://lccn.loc.gov/2022000703
LC ebook record available at https://lccn.loc.gov/2022000704

Book manufactured in Canada

ISBN 9780593354391

1 3 5 7 9 10 8 6 4 2
FRI

Design by Eileen Savage | Text set in Maxime Pro

This book is a work of fiction. Any references to historical events, real people, or real places
are used fictitiously. Other names, characters, places, and events are products of the author's
imagination, and any resemblance to actual events or places or persons, living or dead,
is entirely coincidental.

The publisher does not have any control over and does not assume any responsibility
for author or third-party websites or their content.

This one is for my father, Shashi Walavalkar,
a lifelong Mumbaikar.

Water, water, every where,
And all the boards did shrink;
Water, water, every where,
Nor any drop to drink.

—Samuel Taylor Coleridge

- 1 -

Sanjay and I sit on the top of the hill and stare out at the huge, never-ending Arabian Sea. The salty breeze brings a little relief from the heat.

"It feels like the world is made of water from up here," I say. "That there's enough of it for everyone."

But I know there isn't.

In the distance, the flyover bridge soars into the sky and snakes across the bay. Its lights twinkle and outshine the stars in the night sky.

"The sea link bridge looks like an *M*," I say.

"It does," my brother says. "*M* for Mumbai?"

"*M* for me—Minni," I say. "And for Monsoon. I hope this year we have a good one." Lately the monsoon season comes later and later, which means less and less water.

Although water surrounds my island city, most of the people I know are always struggling to get enough. We don't have running water in our house. We just have a tap outside that we share with our neighbors. Ma has to wake up at the crack of dawn to fill our buckets because the authorities only supply water for two hours every morning and for an hour in the evening when the shortages aren't too bad. The rest of the day, the tap is dry. Every home has a big barrel outside the house, to store collected water for the day.

"Remember when Ma and the other women draped our leaky old tap with a marigold garland as if it was a god they could charm with flowers?" Sanjay says.

I do remember, and we laugh, although it's sad to think it was probably a frustrating day when the water trickled rather than flowed.

I look out at the ocean. Part of our view is blocked by billboards with glamorous Bollywood movie stars—billboards that are larger than our house.

The houses in our neighborhood are small and crammed on top of each other, but they do face the sea. Rich people who live in skyscrapers pay millions for the same ocean view.

Last year, a charity helped paint our homes and fix our leaking tin roofs. Some said it was because the people whizzing past in their air-conditioned cars on the flyover bridge didn't want to see decaying, moldy "slums."

I chose yellow for our house. I helped to sand down the years of moss and mold from our old tin and concrete walls. Baba, Ma, Sanjay, and I dipped our brushes in yellow, and the first coat of paint was like a ray of bright sunshine getting rid of the darkness. My neighbors chose purple and blue, and red and orange. Our street looks like a rainbow.

"Sanjay," I ask, "will we have to worry about water when we are grown up?"

For a long moment, he is silent.

So I answer myself. "No. No, we won't."

I point at the cluster of tall buildings shimmering in the distance where Ma works in the afternoons. I say, "One day, we'll live in one of those tall shiny buildings, where water runs from taps."

"Okay," he says, and links his arm in mine, as if I'm predicting the future. "Like the boy who was born here and studied computers and now has an office in a building and employs sixty people."

I nod.

"Can you imagine," I say, "that on top of some of those high-rise buildings they have a swimming pool full of water? Enough for our whole neighborhood to bathe. How do you think they built a pool on top of a building? Wouldn't you love to see it?"

Sanjay laughs. "You and your questions!"

"Well, they are awfully lucky to have so much water to spare . . ."

"Minni," he says, "I wish there was a way to make all this seawater drinkable. Then there'd be enough for us all."

"There is a way!" I say. "Our teacher told us it's possible—

she said it's called desalination. But it's expensive, and you need a huge factory to strain the salt out."

"Look how smart you are," he says. "You will live in a fancy building!"

"You too," I say.

Sanjay is fifteen, and after he graduated from tenth grade last year, he got a job in a restaurant. He dreams of being a chef, but for now he does food prep. It's good he likes what he's doing, because we didn't have money for college anyway.

I dream for him too. Chef Sanjay.

I pretend to be a palmist and study both our hands.

"Could I be like Meena Aunty?" I ask.

"Why not? Knowing you, you can do anything you set your mind on doing," he says. "And plus you're even named after Ma's sister."

"Like her, I will finish school and get a good job," I wish aloud.

"Hmmm, Minni Meow, banker," he says, teasing me with my childhood nickname. "But I think I see you more as a scientist."

"That'd be cool—or maybe a builder," I say dreamily. "I bet those high-rise roofs don't leak like ours after the monsoon. Wouldn't it be great if ours didn't? And if they didn't get so hot?"

We head home as the sun starts to dip. There is a line for the water tap on the main street. Water pressure must be weak today. When it doesn't get through the web of makeshift hoses, people must line up at the main source. The water line snakes around the block, and we hear the sounds of insults being hurled and see some men shoving one another. There are shrieks. Women scatter. Angry noises fill my ears.

Another fight's breaking out.

We don't wait to see what happens. Sanjay grabs my hand, and we turn around and away from the scene and find our way home through alleys and side streets. My heart thumps along with my running feet.

Our father has told us a million times over the years, *If you invite trouble, it will come. It will stay for chai and for dinner.*

We definitely don't want to invite trouble.

- 2 -

Ma makes the most delicious daal in the world, and my father has eaten two bowls of it. "I might make the best tea and pakodas, but your ma is the greatest at everything else," he says, and sighs in contentment.

Ma blushes whenever Baba praises her cooking.

Ma's potatoes melt in your mouth too, and I've saved a few for the last bite of my meal. Sanjay's right hand hovers over my plate, and I slap it away.

"Minni Meow won't even give me a potato!" he says dramatically.

"Ma," I complain, "tell him to stop calling me that—I'm not five anymore."

But I can't help giggling and give him the bite anyway. I've never been able to resist his goofy ways.

We're seated on the floor in the center of our living space. Curtains separate this from our parents' sleeping area, and

Sanjay and I sleep up in a small loft. Never-ending sounds of honking horns and smells of cooking food and the citronella that keeps away mosquitoes fill the air in our home.

"Something happened today in the water line, and there was another fight," my father tells us. Baba runs a tea shop named Jai Ho, which means "victory." It's where everybody in our neighborhood hangs out, so he hears everything that goes on.

Sanjay and I exchange a look because we know a little too well what Baba is talking about.

We don't mention it because our father also believes in the proverb illustrated by the three monkeys—one with his hands over his eyes, the second with them over his ears, and the third covering his mouth—symbolizing "See no evil, hear no evil, and say no evil."

Ma kisses her Ganesh locket. "I hope no one got hurt."

"The water pressure is too low already," Baba says. "Someone said they might have to order a water tanker. That usually doesn't happen till May."

Ma looks worried. Buying water means money. Money that we don't have.

Then she pulls a flyer from her bag. "This was on the bulletin board at the clinic."

Baba's sitting back in his worn-out wicker chair, but now he straightens up, alert. "Why were you at the clinic?"

"That's not important," she says.

"Yes, it is," Sanjay and I say together.

"My stomach hurt," Ma says. "So I went to see the new doctor, but the line was too long, so I couldn't wait."

I had noticed that Ma didn't seem to have much of an appetite lately.

"It's probably nothing. A little bug probably, like last year. Remember the doctor said we should *always* boil our water," she says.

"We almost always do," Sanjay says. "Are you feeling better?"

"I feel tired, but I'm okay. Now forget about me. I'm glad I went, because otherwise I might not have heard about the computer class," says Ma.

What? Computer class!

My eyes are wide. The small room suddenly feels spacious. It's as if the word *computer*, spoken aloud, has magically created windows in the walls where none existed.

Baba, who is usually a quiet listener, has so many questions. Who is running the class? Where will it be held and when? Who decides who'll get in? What will they teach?

Then Sanjay asks the important question: "Ma, how much does it cost?"

The room shrinks down to size again. Money: It rules everything.

"I don't know," says Ma, "but before leaving for work tomorrow, I will go back and find out."

Ma works hard. Every day, she cooks and cleans not only

for our family, but also for a family that lives in one of the expensive high-rise buildings not far from where we live.

"One of my friends said her son learned computers right after school and got a job in a big office." Ma tousles Sanjay's hair. "Maybe our Sanjay could get a job like that."

"It will be Minni," Sanjay says. "She's the smart one. She's always first in her class. Plus I've got a job already."

"Perhaps you both will," says Ma.

Sanjay is downcast whenever Ma dreams of him getting another job. She doesn't believe in his chef dream like me. I wish she did.

"You'll be a star chef on TV with your own show, Sanjay," I say. "And I'll be in the audience and clap the loudest. They'll name dishes after you. Sanjay's bhindi masala."

Baba laughs affectionately at me. "Minni and her dreams," he says.

Ma jumps up, a big smile on her face. "I almost forgot. I have a surprise. Pinky gave me a mango. An Alphonso mango."

"Those are so expensive!" I say.

"Yes, they are," says Ma. "And the season has barely started."

Ma takes the mango out of her cloth bag and places it on a plate. It isn't overripe. It doesn't have any black or brown spots. It's golden yellow, with streaks of red. Firm to the touch and perfectly ripe, shaped like a kidney. The mango gleams.

Three pairs of eyes turn toward Ma. We need to know more.

Ma giggles like a schoolgirl. Her smile lifts her cheekbones. "Pinky's hair was all in tangles, and it hurt too much when her mother tried to comb it, so I offered to help."

Pinky is the daughter of the family Ma works for, and she's about my age.

I imagine Ma's gentle hand combing through Pinky's hair and braiding it like she does mine.

"And for that she gave you an Alphonso mango?" Sanjay says.

Mama laughs. "You didn't hear how loud Pinky was yelling at her mom. Anita Ma'am said Pinky was giving her a headache."

Ma cuts the juicy fruit into four portions. I notice Ma's portion is smaller than the others, and Sanjay's is just a bit bigger than mine.

"Ma," Sanjay says, "you should comb Pinky's hair every day through the mango season."

"I would do it anytime," Ma says. "Pinky is a sweet girl. And Anita Ma'am's always been good to us, even paying Minni's school fees this year."

I stop mid-bite. "You never told me that," I say.

"I didn't? It was back in December when I needed to send some money to your grandmother and was worried about being able to pay your fees. She offered."

I wrestle with this knowledge. What would we have done if Ma's boss hadn't offered? Would I have been sent to the free government-run school instead of my current school, which is run by an educational charity?

How could Ma not tell me something that important? It's troubling to think my future was in the hands of someone else and I didn't even know.

After dinner I sit outside on our stoop. Moti, the neighborhood dog, who belongs to no one and everyone, comes up to me whimpering. Normally he hangs out at Naan Aunty's house, a couple doors down from us, where he gets handouts of her famous bread. We call her Naan Aunty because she makes the best naans—she bakes hundreds every day for the local shops, and for some fancy restaurants too.

Moti keeps whimpering, which is unusual, so I walk down the lane with him and see Naan Aunty's door is closed and the lights are turned off.

"Moti," I say, "this *is* odd. I wonder where they went."

The older men playing cards at the corner see me. "Naan Aunty's at the clinic with her husband," one of them says. "He was hurt in a fight at the water line."

Nooo!

I race back to tell my parents. Naan Aunty and Ma are

best friends. Uncle is such a meek man, I can't imagine him fighting.

My father leaps to his feet. "Let's go see if they need help."

Cars cannot enter our neighborhood because the streets are too narrow. So we don't worry about being run over as we walk toward the clinic. Instead we look out for bikes and take care to skirt around kids playing cricket, teens rapping, and older folks playing cards or carrom in the middle of the road.

We pass second-shift workers going to work and others returning home. I hear someone memorizing times tables and someone saying evening prayers. In this heat everyone's doors are open, making it easy to know each other's business.

Then I see Naan Aunty and her husband walking toward us. In my excitement, I practically knock over a game board placed on a stool, and everyone shouts, "Minni! Look where you're walking, girl."

"I'm sorry," I say, and I slow down a bit as I race toward Naan Aunty.

Uncle has a gauze bandage around his head, covering his forehead, and leans on Aunty as they take slow steps. They both look exhausted.

"A stone came flying at me," says Uncle. "Hit me right above my eye."

"We were lucky he ducked," says Naan Aunty. "He could have lost an eye."

My father steps forward. "Lean on me," he says to Uncle.

One of the men playing carrom comes and helps on the other side.

I hold Naan Aunty's arm as we walk home. I am so happy Uncle is okay. He didn't invite trouble, but it found him anyway. I guess you can be in the wrong place at the wrong time, so you have to be careful—and lucky.

THAT EVENING, I write in my notebook. Shanti, our friend and neighborhood storyteller, keeps a journal, and she encouraged me to do so as well. We both find it helps untangle our thoughts and calm our minds. I've also discovered I like writing poems, even though Sanjay teases me, calling me Minni Meow, poetess.

Tonight I write:

The water reaches out to the horizon,
as far as my eyes can see.
Sometimes the sea gently rolls,
rocking the fishing boats.
Other days it whirls and rises up,
smashing against the rocks.
They say water is life.
Does it know the trouble it causes?
The fights?
The lines?

The heartache?
Today, though, it's calm.
Beautiful, like yards and yards of a blue sari
woven with threads of silver.
But what will tomorrow bring?

- 4 -

On our way home from school, my best friend, Faiza, and I chatter like we always do, dodging stray dogs, sleeping cows, trash heaps, and street vendors without missing a step or a beat in our conversation.

"Minni," she says, "yesterday, Masterji taught us the dance steps to the song from *Student of the Year*."

"The movie?" I say.

Faiza nods. "I imagined that I was Alia the whole time."

"Why not? You are just as talented as any Bollywood actress," I say.

"You think so?" she asks.

"It's the way you spin and twirl, and your rhythm," I say. "If I tried that, I'd fall on my face."

Faiza reaches for my hand. "You are my best friend. For life."

Which is true. We've known each other forever. We've played hopscotch and fought over dolls. It has never mattered that I'm Hindu and Faiza is Muslim. When Faiza's ammi makes kebabs for Eid, she always saves one for me. When Ma makes ladoos for Diwali, she saves one for Faiza.

When we are almost at the banyan tree, we hear Shanti blowing into her conch shell, so we race over and find her sitting under the tree's canopy. Faiza and I come here often, even when Shanti isn't telling stories. Sometimes the three of us just sit and talk about our world. Shanti's a teacher too and gives the best advice.

This afternoon, a lot of the neighborhood is here. Shanti begins. "Today I'll tell the story of a wedding and a most interesting dowry."

Everyone sighs. Who doesn't like a wedding?

We got to go to one last summer when our neighbor Reva got married. Faiza and I danced till our feet had blisters. They served the softest, sweetest jalebis at the feast, which burst into syrupy sweetness in my mouth. If I close my eyes, I can see the deep red sari that Reva wore, and the beautiful henna etched onto her hands.

The small crowd that has gathered is as excited as we are.

"Was there a song and dance party before the wedding?" asks Faiza. "It's not a wedding without a sangeet."

Yes! Yes! Everyone agrees.

"Shush," says Shanti. "This was a long-ago wedding and a different kind—a royal one. King John of Portugal's daughter, Catherine of Braganza, was to be married to Charles II of England. What do you think King John gave as a dowry?"

"A refrigerator?" I say.

"A car?" Faiza says.

"A house?" That's Sanjay's voice. He's joined the crowd too.

Shanti laughs her wonderful huge laugh.

"This was four hundred years ago—there were no fridges or cars back then, and Charles II probably had all the palaces he needed. So King John promised Bombay to the British as part of Catherine's dowry." Shanti pauses again like a good storyteller.

"Bombay? The city we live in? Who gives a city?" I ask.

"Kings do!" says Shanti.

"Was Bombay King John's to give?" someone shouts out.

Shanti blows into her conch shell, and when the crowd quiets, she says, "Back then the city was seven disconnected islands, floating in one big swamp."

"Swamp?" someone asks.

"Yes, this was all swamp back then," Shanti answers. "So they gathered rocks, and they dumped them by the boatload into the sea."

"Then what happened?" someone says.

"The rocks were bigger than men," Shanti says. "And they built a wall to push back the sea. But the sea was having none of it. The sea crumbled the wall again and again."

If I close my eyes, I can see that wall collapse, like homes and roofs do during a fierce monsoon.

When Shanti winds up her story, Fazia has a question. "Were the people who lived on the islands part of the dowry?" she asks. "Were we like cattle, of no importance back then?"

"We aren't exactly important now either," says Sanjay. "Which is why we don't get water. And get questioned before we enter fancy shops. As if we might steal."

"You are bringing up an important point," Shanti says, using her best teacher voice.

To LIGHTEN THE mood as we walk home, Faiza breaks out some of the new dance steps she learned.

"Nice moves," Sanjay says. "When you become a dancer in a Bollywood film, don't forget that I taught you how to hold a cricket bat."

"When you become a big-time chef, don't forget that I taught you how to dance a little better than you used to, which isn't saying much." Faiza laughs.

Amit, Sanjay's friend, comes running toward us, excited. "Sanjay, my uncle has that new car tonight. He said we could go for a ride."

Amit's uncle Ram is a chauffeur, and his employers travel a lot and are always needing to be dropped off or picked up at the airport.

Sanjay is excited. "I'm in—that moonroof is cool! And I bet the sound system is too."

"It is, and there are TVs on the back of the seats too." Amit sees my eyes light up, and he turns to me and raps:

"Ahh, Minni, the seats are made of butter-soft leather. Never sat on anything better. AC blasts out super icy 'cause this car's the kind that's pricey. Any day I can I'm gonna glide in my uncle's borrowed ride."

"That's so cool, Amit. You can make a rhyme about *anything*," Faiza says. "Can Minni and I come too?"

"I don't know if I can twist Ram Uncle's arm," Amit says.

"Please, please, please? I'll teach you some dance moves." She tilts her head, and her eyes look like Moti's when he wants a naan.

"Okay, okay, I'll try. How can I say no?" Amit grins. "Meet us after dinner, and I'll try to convince my uncle to let you come."

"You'll thank me when you become a rap star," Faiza yells as we leave. "It's good to have some moves."

"She's right," I add. "Faiza will help you dance like Shah Rukh Khan—then you can be the next king of Bollywood. You won't regret it."

"King Amit! Okay, I'm down with it," Amit shouts back as he disappears into the night.

- 5 -

"It's a brand-new Mercedes," Ram Uncle is saying with pride. Then he sees me and Faiza. "Why are they here?" he asks Amit. "I told you one friend. You think I can give rides to all the kids in the neighborhood?"

"Sorry, Uncle," Amit says. "It's just that these girls work so hard, and I thought maybe you could give them a treat . . ." He gets in the front seat.

Amit's uncle doesn't look convinced, and I step back, ready to turn around and go home, but Faiza grabs my arm and whispers, "Not so soon."

"Uncle," she says in her sweetest voice, "I've never been in a Mercedes. Does it have cold air? Are the seats made of leather?"

Silence. One . . . two . . . three . . . four . . . five . . . six . . .

Amit's uncle sighs. "Okay, okay, get in, but don't touch anything."

Sanjay, Faiza, and I scramble into the back seat before

Uncle can change his mind. Then he turns the key, and we feel the throb of the powerful engine. He rolls the windows up and presses a button. A blast of cold air hits us and gives us shivers.

We are quiet for a bit, looking out at Mumbai at night. Then the roof of the car starts to open with a whooshing sound, and we can see the sky. Uncle sees our amazed faces. "Go on," he says. "Stand up, push your head out through the roof, and look at the world."

He doesn't need to tell us twice. We kick off our flip-flops, stand on the seat, and poke our heads out. Sanjay raises his hands high and yells, "Mumbai! I'm Sanjay."

The night air is still hot and sticky, so the wind feels good. I raise my hands too, and in that moment it feels like I could conquer the world. Too soon, we hear Uncle's voice. "Enough! Come in."

The roof closes. Our laughter fills the car, and then Uncle turns on the radio and we sing along to the newest Bollywood song.

The car slows down, and Uncle says he needs to make a stop, pointing to a building. He says he'll be back in ten minutes. "Stay in the car."

Once he leaves, Sanjay scrambles into the front seat with Amit. The radio's off, but we continue to sing the song. Sanjay is so loud, his voice drowns out ours.

"Hey," Amit says, "what's going on out there?"

We all peer through the car windows and across the iron fence, where we see the Western railway tracks. Behind the tracks there's a huge water tanker truck. The kind the community orders when the water shortages get really bad and nothing runs from our taps.

"Why is a truck back there? Nobody lives there," says Faiza.

Amit opens the driver's door. "I'm going to check it out."

"Wait!" I say. "Your uncle said to stay in the car."

But Amit doesn't seem to care. "I'm just going as far as the fence—it's in the shadows, so no one can see us. It will be okay."

I can't believe Amit is disobeying his uncle, but Sanjay always said he was a daredevil. What I didn't expect is Sanjay getting out of the car too. "Sanjay, don't," I say, but he doesn't listen.

"Just for a minute," he says.

Faiza sees how upset I am and repeats what Amit said. "It'll be okay. Don't worry."

But I can't help it. I hear Baba's voice in my head about inviting trouble. This feels wrong.

For a few minutes Amit and Sanjay stand by the fence, and then Amit begins climbing over. Sanjay follows. How could he? Doesn't Sanjay remember *anything* Baba has taught us?

I feel trapped in the car and need to get air, so I open the door and step out. *Be careful,* I want to yell to the boys, but I don't. Something tells me I should not draw attention to them. Once over the fence, they crouch and cross the tracks in the shadows and hide behind some bushes.

Faiza is standing with me. "Why did they cross the tracks?" Now Faiza's voice is nervous too.

"What if Uncle comes back and they are stuck on the other side while the train's passing?" I whisper to Faiza.

Now that my eyes have adjusted to the dark, I see that a hose attached to the tanker truck is draining water from the pipeline that runs near the tracks.

Faiza whispers, "Minni, why are they taking the water?"

It's a hot March night, but I shiver. In the distance we hear a train whistle.

We hear the voice of an angry man. "Pay attention, you knucklehead. I'm not paying you to chat with your friends. Hurry up."

Then I hear Sanjay sneeze—and the man shouts, "Hey, who's out there? Who are you? You from one of those newspapers or the police? Or just little rats?"

The angry man gets closer, aiming his flashlight near the bushes where Sanjay and Amit are still hiding. In the glare of the light, I can see the man has a scar on his cheek.

We watch as he grabs Sanjay. But Amit comes from behind and kicks the man hard on his leg. The man yelps in pain, and when he lets go of Sanjay, the boys race away.

"Ravi," the man shouts to one of his workers, "catch the rascals."

By now we can hear the click-clacking of train wheels. It's coming fast and looks like a racing dragon with its flaring headlights. Will it block Sanjay and Amit's pathway back to us?

I instinctively shut my eyes. I want to see no evil, but it is happening right in front of us.

I squeeze my hands together and pray.

- 6 -

When I look up, the boys are jumping over the fence.

They beat the train!

Faiza and I hold the car doors open for Sanjay and Amit, and we all pile in. The boys are panting, and their faces gleam with sweat. Sanjay has scratches on his hands.

A minute later Ram Uncle returns, just as the train disappears.

As he gets into the car, we can hear the angry man shouting, "I will catch those boys! I'm gonna get them!"

Ram Uncle looks at our terrified faces, hears the yelling man, starts the car, and speeds away. When we've driven for a few minutes, I exhale.

Ram Uncle pulls the car over when we are near home. "Amit," he says, "what happened?"

"Nothing," Amit says.

"Is that why you boys look like you saw a ghost?" he asks.

No one answers.

"Is that why that man was yelling and threatening?" he shouts. His voice bounces off the walls of the car.

I speak up. "Ram Uncle, they went to see what was going on with a water truck."

"Why?" He bangs his hands against the steering wheel. "Is it your business? Are you the police?"

"No," both Amit and Sanjay say.

"We didn't know. We were just curious," Sanjay says.

Ram Uncle laughs, a scary laugh. "You were *curious?* You're fifteen—don't you know you can't afford to be curious about everything? You can be curious about what your mother's cooking for dinner or what your friends are doing after school. Not about what tankers are doing in the night. You need to remember there are times when it is best to keep your head down and go about your business."

Ram Uncle sounds exactly like Baba.

"Did anyone recognize you?" he asks.

"There was a guy from our neighborhood," says Amit.

"His name is Ravi, and he works for the government," says Sanjay. "But he's a good guy. He told us to run for it right before the train came."

Ram Uncle shakes his head, starts the car up, and we head on home. No one dares to say another word. None of us care about the moonroof, or the music system, or the TV on the back of the seat. If only we had just stayed in the car.

"Let's hope that the boss forgets about you boys. You both were very lucky that Ravi was there. You all will not utter a word about this to anyone, understand?" Ram Uncle says.

We scramble out of the car. Faiza and I hug each other hard. She lays a hand on Sanjay's shoulder and says, "It'll be okay."

Will it, though?

Sanjay and I walk home through the maze of lanes in silence. Barely an hour ago we felt lucky—not anymore.

Outside the house, I wash the dirt off Sanjay with my damp handkerchief. We creep into the house, and fortunately our parents are asleep behind their curtain.

We climb the ladder into our loft and spread out our bedrolls as quietly as possible. Our home is so small that there's no room for secrets. We found that out when we were young and our mother seemed to know everything that I'd whispered to Sanjay the night before. She knew that Faiza had given me a whole chocolate bar and I had only saved a small, melty square for Sanjay. She knew that I was angry with her when she made me eat okra. I sometimes think she sleeps with one ear open, and it amazes me that she can hear anything besides our father snoring!

But we were smart kids, and we found a way to share secrets by using a notebook. I get one out now and write:

what's going to happen?
I don't know ☹ I'm sorry, Minni.

what do you think they were doing there?

Looked like they were stealing water.

Then Sanjay pushes the notebook back to me. He curls up into a ball and closes his eyes.

I begin to pray, asking Lord Ganesh to help and protect us. But then I remember I need to be grateful too. For a moment when the train was coming, I imagined the angry man really hurting Sanjay. I imagined the train crushing him.

We came close, too close, to evil. Those thoughts make my toes curl. So I thank God one more time that my brother is beside me in our loft, under this roof, inhaling and exhaling.

- 7 -

Sanjay and I wake up and try to pretend like last night didn't happen. Maybe in a year we might all laugh about our adventure, but today the memory is as heavy as the full bucket of water that I haul in for Ma. It weighs me down. When Sanjay sees the dread on my face as I do my chores, he whispers, "Minni, Ma will suspect something. Stop."

But I'm not a good actress like Faiza. I eat my roti with ghee and jam as Ma braids my hair.

"You're quiet today," she remarks. "No stories about Faiza or your teacher or Shanti?"

When I answer with a shake of my head, she touches my forehead to make sure I don't have a fever.

When her back is turned, Sanjay glares at me. *Smile,* he mimes, and I try.

Faiza meets me at our corner, and we are both tense as we walk to school. On the way, I stop before a makeshift temple under a tree to pray. A Ganesh idol carved out of stone is lodged near the base of the tree, and the elephant's head is draped in marigold garlands. Bells hang above it, and I clang them twice for good measure.

"What did you pray for?" Faiza asks.

"I prayed that the man forgets about Sanjay and Amit. That he decides they were just foolish boys who meant no harm and wandered where they shouldn't."

"Me too!" says Faiza. "That's what I've been praying."

AT SCHOOL, AS much as I want to, I can't erase the threats of the angry man, and they continue to ring in my ears. Our teacher, Miss Shah, always starts the day with math problems. I copy them down in my notebook like a robot. I usually like math, but today I can hardly add up the numbers.

Faiza, at the next desk, is struggling too. She has erased most of her page, and it looks like there are gray clouds on it. In frustration, she swipes harder, and the page rips.

On the way home from school, we see Uncle's Mercedes parked on the main street, close to our side street. "Why has he come here?" I ask Faiza. "Is he telling my parents?"

I pick up my pace. I'm almost running. Faiza is too.

I push the door open and see Ma, Baba, Sanjay, Amit, and his uncle. They all barely fit in our house. Ma's face is streaked with tears. I've never seen Baba look so angry—a vein near his temple throbs. Sanjay and Amit look at their feet. Amit's uncle is holding a newspaper folded open to an article. He keeps raising the newspaper as he talks, and I manage to read the headline: MUMBAI RULED BY WATER MAFIA. I've never heard of the water mafia before.

"There she is. The keeper of her brother's secrets," Ma says through clenched teeth.

When she sees Faiza behind me, she says, "Beti, please go home now," and then closes the door.

We never completely close our front door during the day. It makes the house unbearably hot.

Right now, it feels like we've also trapped fear and anger and disappointment inside.

Uncle says, "We need to send the boys away for a while—till things blow over."

Silence.

"These people," he says, pointing to the newspaper, "these water mafia people are dangerous."

"Send them where?" I ask.

"Uncle's brother lives near New Delhi," my father says. "He and his family work on a farm."

Amit says, "But we didn't do anything."

"You did enough," Uncle says angrily, and lifts his hand as if he will strike Amit for speaking.

Baba puts a hand on Uncle's shoulder to calm him.

"My friends have heard that the man Ravi was working

for last night has been talking about you," Uncle says. "He thinks you boys are spies for the newspapers or part of a rival gang."

Baba and the boys look scared.

I'm stunned. None of us knows what to say.

"These people are dangerous," Uncle repeats. "They sell the water they steal for a big profit."

Ma asks the question that none of us dares to ask: "What will happen if they come for Sanjay and Amit?"

"Nothing good," Baba and Uncle say together.

"Maybe we should go to the police," I say.

The adults look at me like I've lost my mind. Uncle turns to Ma. "Teach her something before she gets in trouble."

"Who will listen to us?" Baba says. "We're considered uneducated slum dwellers. We don't speak English. And the water mafia's been known to bribe the police."

I move closer to Sanjay. As if that will somehow make a difference.

Sanjay looks at his toes and mumbles, "I don't want to put my family in danger. I'll leave."

Amit nods in agreement. He's on the verge of tears. All his boldness and bluster are gone.

It's decided. Amit and Sanjay will leave on the train for Delhi tonight. Then they will take a bus. Uncle's relative will meet them there and take them to the farm, where they can work for him.

There isn't much time. Uncle will be back in a few hours to take the boys to the train station.

None of this feels real.

BABA HAS A suitcase, and I help to pack Sanjay's clothes.

Ma empties out the savings she has in the cupboard. She counts the money. It's enough for a ticket and maybe a few meals.

Ma has made dinner. But none of us can eat.

She tries to feed Sanjay some roti and potatoes, and when he refuses, she says, "Eat, beta. I don't know when I'll be able to cook for you again."

"I don't want to leave." Sanjay's voice shakes. "I've never left Mumbai except to go to your village."

"You should've thought of that before you poked your nose where you shouldn't," says Ma.

Ma talks tough when she is angry and hopeless. And after that outburst, nobody says a word. All I can think about is that I don't know when I will see my brother again.

Uncle arrives and says, "Say goodbyes quickly. We need to get to the train station, and there's traffic. I've got to meet my employer at the airport tonight and can't be late."

We all give Sanjay a hug, and then Ma puts her phone in his pocket.

"No, Ma," says Sanjay. "You need it."

She puts her hands on Sanjay's shoulders. He is taller than

she is. "I need to hear your voice and know that you are safe even more. I can borrow a phone to call you."

And then he is gone.

I sit on the stoop that evening, stroking Moti's fur. "Moti, I miss my brother already. I've never lived a day without him."

Moti understands. He looks at me with mournful eyes.

- 8 -

The house feels so empty without Sanjay.

I try to do homework. It's hard to focus, but I need to because finals are in April—just a month away. If I don't pass, I don't go to the next grade. There are more stories of kids who flunk out than I want to hear. When they fail, they stop going to school and have to take any job they can to start earning money to help their families. Some girls get married.

For me, these are not just stories, they are what happened to my neighbors and my own parents.

Baba was in sixth grade when his father hurt his back. He got a job to help the family and never had a chance to go back to school. Ma left school when her youngest sister was born; she was the oldest and had to take care of her.

I. Can't. Flunk. Out.

I open my math book.

If a train leaves Mumbai, travels at 105 kilometers an
hour, and goes north toward Delhi, which is 1,421 kilome-
ters away, how long will it take to reach Delhi?

All I can imagine is Sanjay on that train. He's never been
on a long-distance one before. I imagine it's very different
from our Mumbai subway, which stops every five minutes.
The one time we left Mumbai to go to our grandmother's village, we took the bus. One of our favorite games was guess-
ing where the trains we passed were going. Delhi, Shimla,
Bangalore, Calcutta. We imagined them going to all the
places we hadn't been, which was everywhere.

Even recently, when planes flew overhead, Sanjay and I
would imagine being in one. One day Sanjay told me, "See
that plane in the sky? They serve lunch and dinner on the
plane. They even have bedrooms, and you can sleep all night
before you land in another country."

Faiza was with us that day, and we both burst out laughing. "Who told you that? Now, that's a lie!" I said.

I read the problem again. The letters blur through unshed
tears. I know I need to use the time formula.

$T = D / S$.

I need to put in the numbers and calculate. Today I do the
problem because I need to know when Sanjay and Amit will
reach Delhi.

At night, I spread my bedroll horizontally instead of

vertically. I'm alone up here. I don't have to share space. I stare at the pictures on our wall. They are ripped pages from old magazines. Sanjay's are all pictures of mouthwatering food. Golden samosas and chicken korma.

Mine are of places I find beautiful, mostly beaches. There's also a picture of me tying a bracelet on Sanjay's wrist to protect him from harm. I had made the rakhi bracelet myself after Shanti taught me how.

I lie down and stretch my legs. Baba has not returned. It's just Ma and me, so Baba's rhythmic snoring can't lull me to sleep.

The notebook under my pillow might as well be a rock. It reminds me that I can't write messages for Sanjay and he isn't here to write back and fight and argue.

I replay our hurried hug and goodbye. "You'll write to me sometimes, won't you?" he asked.

I know he likes to act like he is all strong, but Sanjay is fifteen. The world is huge, and more dangerous than either of us thought.

If only Sanjay had listened to me. I start feeling angry at him again. When he is with Amit, he sure has a knack for getting into trouble. A few summers ago, the two of them decided the best way to travel was jumping from roof to roof, since the roads were crowded with people and the houses were close together.

Sanjay would say, "I feel like Superman and Hanuman rolled into one when I'm jumping."

"But you're not Superman, and you're not the flying monkey god either," I warned him. "You're a flesh-and-blood human and will get hurt."

Sanjay was lucky, but Amit did fall. He sprained his ankle and had to hobble around with a brace on his foot. Baba said, "You boys didn't just invite trouble in, you begged for it."

I toss and turn. At around two A.M., Baba comes in from his shop, and in a few minutes he starts snoring.

Still, my brain won't stop spinning. It churns like the sea during a storm. Finally, I find my journal. A few years ago I had to write *I will not talk in class* a hundred times as a punishment. Today I write *Please, please, Sanjay, stay safe.*

I write it again and again and again. Today it feels like a wish, a prayer.

- 9 -

Next morning, Faiza is at my doorstep instead of meeting me at our usual place.

"Where's Sanjay?" she says. "What happened?"

In my misery I've forgotten she doesn't know.

"The grown-ups decided that Amit and Sanjay should go away for a while," I whisper.

"Go away? What do you mean, go away?" Faiza's voice is raised.

I reach for her hand and squeeze. "Shh! We have to be careful. If anyone asks, we say he went to the village to help my grandparents."

"Did he?" she whispers.

I weigh my choices. If Sanjay is my brother, Faiza is my sister. It doesn't matter that we have different mothers or believe in different gods. I cannot get through this time alone. I need her. Plus I know she can keep a secret. So I tell her the truth.

When I show her the newspaper that Ram Uncle left behind, her eyes get wide. She's as alarmed as I was when I read about the water mafia. They steal water from wells, pipelines, and tankers in the middle of the night. They bribe the authorities so that they will ignore their wrongdoing. They make huge profits from the misery of others. Without water, people can't live. How can they be so greedy?

Faiza usually has a lot to say, but now she can barely mumble. "I'm scared, Minni."

I reach for her hand. I can't say aloud how terrified I am. I have to keep reminding myself that my brother is smart. "We have to believe in him," I tell Faiza. "Also, he is safe there."

ON OUR WALK to school, I notice a flyer on a lamppost.

Water is life. Stealing water is a crime.

My eyes flicker over every word and the picture of the world held in human hands. Half of the earth is green and lush. The other half is parched, dry, and dying.

The poster is peeling at the corners. How have I not seen it before? What else did I not notice?

Faiza reads my mind. "I never noticed it either," she says, shaking her head.

I think back to all the hard lessons I've learned over the years. When I was little, Ma told me not to touch the stove or I'd get burned. I pricked my finger and realized roses come with thorns. Baba made sure I didn't wander off in a crowd because bad things could happen.

Is this growing up? Learning how dangerous the whole world can be? Learning that not everyone follows the rules. That some people don't care if they hurt others. That they only care about themselves and making a profit.

We reach school and hurry in and take our seats as the bell rings.

Miss Shah hands out packets. "This packet is to help you prepare for the final exam, which is less than a month away."

Loud groans meet her announcement.

"I know," she says. "I'm trying to help. If you study and can answer all the questions in this packet, I promise that you will pass the exam and make it to eighth grade."

Our eyes meet, and she smiles. "I even expect to see some of you go to college."

I blush. I am happy Miss Shah believes in me—and I've always wanted to make it to college too. But now I have to make it through this worrisome time.

I stare out the classroom window. This is a bad time for me to be so distracted—instead of studying, all I can thinking about is what Sanjay might be doing on the farm. Are there other workers besides him and Amit? Where do they live? Sleep? Eat? I wish I could talk to him, but he's so far away.

That night I write to Sanjay instead of writing in my journal. I don't mention the flyer. Instead, I tell him about school, and Faiza, and his friends. Then I add a poem, because when he calls me a poetess, it always makes me smile.

I didn't say namaste
or smile at Trouble
or invite it home.
I didn't recognize it.
Like Red Riding Hood
didn't recognize the wolf.

- 10 -

A week after Sanjay leaves, we are adjusting to our new normal. I miss him, but at least we know he's okay. Sanjay finally called us last night from the farm. It was good to hear his voice, even though the connection was full of static, since the farm is so far from any city.

Ma and I were so relieved to hear his voice that we started to cry—and even Baba had to blink away tears.

"Minni, it's really nice here in the country. The air smells different, and we grow vegetables that get sold in the bazaar," Sanjay told us.

"The air? How so?" I asked.

"It smells fresh—like the earth after rain. It smells of the apples growing on the tree."

"Now who's the poet?" I said. "Tell me more."

"Okay, it smells of okra, your favorite vegetable, Minni."

"Ma made okra yesterday. It was *not* like yours."

I never liked okra till Sanjay cooked it. He sliced it thin

and magically made it crispy and salty and sweet, which made me forget I was even eating okra. When will Sanjay cook for me again?

Sanjay went on to tell us that there was a river nearby— one unlike the dirty Mithi River near our house—where he and some of the other workers go to swim.

I told him I saw some people picking up litter near our river a few days ago. "Maybe I'll join them next time," I said. "Imagine ever being able to swim in the Mithi!"

"That would take a good imagination," Sanjay said. "But if you're helping, who knows?"

After we ended the call, I missed Sanjay more than ever.

I had promised to keep writing, and he promised to try to call again in a week. We were both trying so hard to be brave, but it felt like all our promises were soaked in worry and longing.

So now I have to adjust to life without Sanjay—not just for the fun stuff like reading comic books together and writing silly notes, but for chores too. Sanjay was there each morning to help pour the buckets of water into our big storage barrel and to haul extra water on laundry day. He was stronger than Ma or me. Without him, we struggle and slosh precious water on ourselves.

THAT EVENING, I'M at the neighborhood store picking up a few groceries when I see Ravi. Our eyes meet, and there is a flash of recognition before we both look away.

Should I have said hello?

"Minni," says the shopkeeper. "I haven't seen Sanjay. Where is he?"

A few days ago, I would've answered her simple question with an honest answer. "At work" or "playing cricket."

But now I'm not sure what to say. And Ravi is standing right here, although I know he helped Sanjay and Amit, so he's on our side.

Finally, I mumble, "He had to go help my grandmother for a while."

From the corner of my eye, I see Ravi give the smallest of nods as he walks away.

Moti follows me home. I can tell he misses Sanjay too. He sniffs around, then pokes his head into the house and barks as if calling Sanjay.

After restlessly pacing, he whimpers and looks into my eyes. "I know," I say. "I miss him too."

He sighs, and we settle down together out on the front stoop, Moti's head resting on my foot. I stroke him to comfort myself.

This new normal will never feel right.

- 11 -

When I get home from school the next day, I'm surprised to find Ma there when she should be at work.

Even stranger is that she's asleep. Ma never naps during the day.

I grab a banana, go up to the loft as quietly as possible, and take out my work. But Ma awakens anyway, and I know she is truly sick because she says, "Minni, will you walk with me to the clinic?"

I race down from my loft. "Of course!" I tell her. "What is it?"

"I think I've got a virus again," she says.

Last year when Ma fell sick, the doctor said it was from the water—and now we always boil and strain it to kill the germs. But I think it's odd that nobody else in the family has gotten ill. It makes me worry that it could be something more serious.

As we walk to the clinic, she leans on my arm. The sun

bears down on us, and I can see her forehead is dotted with sweat as she shuffles her feet.

There is a long line at the clinic. Ma is so weak and tired that we sit on the floor as we wait.

Finally the doctor can see us. She is new here and seems kind. She examines Ma and says Ma is probably right—that she's picked up some kind of virus from contaminated food or water.

But when she reads through Ma's chart, I can see she gets more worried. "You've had stomach viruses three times in the last two years, so I'm going to draw blood and do some tests. In the meantime, you are to rest for a week or two. I know it's difficult, but there is no other option."

She gives Ma some medicine to settle her stomach and lets us know she will be in touch when they get the tests back.

"Ma," I say on the walk home. "You need to rest, and I'm going to make sure you do. I'll stay home tomorrow."

"No!" says Ma. Her voice is firm. "You help me in the morning, but you can't miss school. I'll manage."

That evening, I don't leave Ma's side.

When Faiza stops by, Ma is resting, and we sit on the stoop and keep our voices low.

"Faiza," I say, "what is going on? Why are so many bad things happening to my family?"

"I don't know," she says. "But I prayed for all of you and asked Allah for blessings."

"I'm afraid to leave her tomorrow, but that means I'll miss school."

"Then I will take the best notes in the whole world, Minni."

When I roll my eyes and chuckle at that idea, Faiza mock punches me in the arm. "I will. Just for you."

We both know Faiza's easily distracted and her mind always wanders to her songs and dance steps. But I also know that she's the best friend a girl can have, and that she'll try as hard as she can.

"Faiza, you *will* take the best notes, for me and for *you*," I say, and she squeezes my hand.

"At least Sanjay is happy." I let out a sigh. "He really likes living in the country and farming. He told me the family he lives with grows all kinds of vegetables."

"Like what?"

"Tomatoes and cauliflower and carrots and spinach and okra."

"Have you ever seen a vegetable farm?" she asks.

I shake my head. "Only the tomatoes that Shanti grows in a pot. The farm must be pretty. Sanjay says the air is fresh with so much open space and without so many people and cars. I'm glad he likes it there, but I sure do miss him."

I sigh again, and Faiza tugs my braid.

"Is that to remind me of Sanjay?" I ask. She grins and pulls it again.

When we hear Ma moving around inside, Faiza says, "Hey, I learned a song your ma might like. It's from an old movie."

We step inside, and Faiza begins to sing a song about spring. Ma starts to hum along, and her sweet voice fills me with hope.

When it's time for Faiza to leave, I give her a big hug and thank her for making Ma smile.

I'm feeling a little more cheerful until I give Ma her medication and touch her brow.

She is burning up with fever, a symptom she never had before.

- 12 -

I wake up in the morning and make some chai for Ma. She likes ginger and it's good for her stomach, so I grate some in. Baba has left early as usual, so it's up to me to make sure she's okay. I'm relieved that her forehead is cool—and Ma says she feels better.

I'm packing my books when I see Ma stand up, wobble, and reach for the wall for support. Without it, she would have fallen.

"Ma," I say. "Today you listen to me. It's my turn to take care of you." I'm ready to have her argue with me, but instead, she slides back onto her mat.

I hope Faiza will guess that I'm taking care of Ma today when I don't show up.

"Minni," she says. "Go and see if there's water. We are late already. Hope it's not gone."

I take the buckets out to the tap, twist it open, and exhale.

There is water! It's a thin stream, and it takes a while to fill the buckets, but I manage.

Next I need to boil the water. While it's heating, I get my history book so I can study while I wait. I sit near the open door, where there's the most air. But instead of studying, I mostly daydream about living in a house with windows and running water—would that be too much to ask?

I keep checking the pot, but the water stays as still as ever, even though the flame is dancing and blue. Does it always take this long to boil? I don't know because Ma takes care of the water every morning.

When I finally see the first faint bubbles emerge in the pot, I hop on my feet as if I'm cheering a runner to the finish line. "You did it, water!"

While I strain it, I think about what the other doctor at the clinic had explained to us last year when Ma fell sick. That we needed to purify the water like this—*every* day, because even though we can't see them, there are germs in the water that can make us sick. The whole process is so long that I see why it's so easy to skip some days.

Afterward I force myself to go back to my studies. Failing my exam is not an option if I want to get a job that pays well.

When Ma wakes up a few hours later, she sits up and says she feels better. "Minni, you will learn to make rotis."

"Ma, I'm studying. And you've already taught me," I tell her.

"Yes, but I haven't shared all my secrets, and your rotis need to be perfect circles," she says.

My first attempts were shaped like anything but circles.

"The secret is in the dough," Ma says, "and in making sure it doesn't stick to the rolling board. Come on, now. We'll both make a batch."

When Ma makes this bread, she never measures out the flour, except in fistfuls. Now she shows me exactly how much to use. Then she teaches me to build a flour well in a shallow dish. In the center of the well, I add a pinch of salt. Next, Ma teaches me how to add water slowly and incorporate the flour until a ball of dough is formed. Then it's time to drizzle oil and knead the ball.

For some reason, my ball isn't as smooth and easy to knead as hers.

"Minni, this is important." Her voice sounds urgent.

"Why is this so important? Why now?" I ask.

"I'll tell you when Baba comes home," she says.

And later, when Baba comes home, Ma says she has an announcement. "I've decided that I will leave tomorrow and go to the village, where my mother and my youngest sister can care for me."

When both of us open our mouths to speak, she raises her palm at us. "Let me finish," she says.

"I've been lying here thinking all day," she continues. "I need a real rest so I stop falling sick all the time. And, Minni, you need to be in school, not home taking care of me. You need to pass your exam. Plus I will get better faster in the village, where the air is cleaner. And where I know my sister will be happy to make all my favorite dishes."

I look toward Baba, expecting him to object. But his head is bent. "Minni, your mother is right."

"The most important part—I will ask Anita Ma'am to let Minni take my place. After school, instead of coming home, Minni will go there."

I'm so shocked, I'm speechless.

Ma laughs. "My Minni, without words?"

"I've never done a job in a memsahib's house," I say. "I don't know how."

"You're a smart girl, and I'll tell you all you need to know. I already taught you how to make my rotis."

So that's what the cooking lesson was about.

"Can't you tell her you will be back in a month?" Baba asks.

"No," Ma says firmly. "No, I can't do that."

"Why not?" I dare to ask.

"Because she might hire someone else. Then when I return, I'll have no job."

We are all silenced. How do we argue with that?

The room suddenly feels more airless than ever. And I feel like I'm suffocating.

Once again, my future's not in my hands.

Again it seems to be in Anita Ma'am's.

Hands that I've never touched or known.

- 13 -

"**When you ring** their doorbell each day, remember you are not you, our daughter, Sanjay's sister. You are not the girl with so much to say," Ma says.

I'm not sure where this is going. Ma's bags are packed, and Baba has bought her bus ticket. She will leave late this afternoon and travel through most of the night, arriving at dawn. Ma is weak but no longer running a fever, so she can make the journey.

Ma is sipping the tea I made her.

"Minni," she says. "Are you listening?"

I'm half listening and reading my notes.

"Minni, this is as important as your passing the exam," she says.

I whip my head up. What could be as important? Only Sanjay coming back or Ma getting better so she doesn't have to leave.

"Minni," she says, "when you cross the threshold and enter Anita Ma'am's house, you are a servant."

I put my book down and look at my mother. "I get it, Ma—it's a job. I'm working for them."

"Yes, you are," Ma says. "And, Minni—this is crucial—you will need to remember that you cannot have an opinion in that house. You are there to follow orders. You will do as they ask."

"What if they ask me to not peel the onions before cooking them?" I say, hoping to make Ma laugh.

Ma manages a smile but says, "Then you won't. But they do have a cook. I'm usually only asked to make rotis, since Anita Ma'am likes my flatbread so much."

"Well, she has good taste. I like them too." I try to keep Ma smiling, but she is all business.

"Minni, you will speak only when you are asked a question. Oh, and sometimes the question doesn't need an answer, in which case, you won't answer."

I don't understand what she means, but I tuck her advice away.

Ma continues. "And if someone insults you or shouts at you, you don't answer back, unless you want to lose our job."

What is Ma saying? Is this what she goes through every day? She's insulted and treated like a doormat, and then comes home to me and Sanjay quarreling. Why didn't we know this? No wonder she comes home so weary.

"Ma, don't worry. I will work hard and keep the job for you. I promise."

That evening Baba comes home early. He has asked someone to mind the tea stall for him.

One of our neighbors is a taxi driver, and he takes us to the bus depot. It's busy and loud and smells of fried food and diesel fumes. People rush around saying goodbyes—some with laughter, others with tears. There is a large group singing songs and carrying a sign that says MARRIAGE PARTY.

There are several buses, and we find Ma's. She hugs me close and holds me tight. I hug her back. I want to say *Please don't go*, but that would be useless.

"You need to grow up, Minni," she says. "I'm sorry."

She gets on the bus, takes her seat, and then reaches down through the open window to hold Baba's and my hands. "I will use my sister's phone and call you when I can."

Baba and I watch as the bus hurtles off, leaving clouds of fumes behind.

I want to shout to the departing bus, and at the world.

If growing up means not having my mother or brother around, I don't want any part of it.

Too bad I don't have a choice.

- 14 -

Baba and I return home in silence. We've never been by ourselves. Years ago, when Ma went to visit her family for a week, Sanjay was with us.

I'm overcome by the emptiness in our little house.

My breath feels tight, and I stare out the window. Ma's basil plant is wilted, so I water it. Every once in a while, Sanjay would climb the ladder and sit on our house's tin roof. He said he felt like a king with a view of the vast endless ocean and everything beyond the horizon. For Sanjay, climbing the ladder felt like an adventure. For me it felt scary, so I rarely joined him.

The ladder to the roof is rusty. It's also coming loose where it's nailed to the wall, so that when you step on it, it wobbles. But that never stopped Sanjay, and it won't stop me.

Ma said I need to grow up, and I decide I'll try to be more fearless. I want to replace my aloneness with courage. I will climb up and try to feel like a king too.

I step on the first rung of the ladder and feel it shake. I grip both sides, clench my jaw, and lift my foot to the next rung, then I do it again and again until I'm up on the roof. Now it's my knees that are shaking, and I'm scared when I look down. But the blood pumping to my heart tells me that I made it. I open my eyes wide and look ahead. The view is amazing. And I do feel like a king because I conquered my fear.

I scramble back down.

I REMEMBER THE one person who knows how it feels to stand tall and strong alone—Shanti. After her husband and daughter died in an accident many years ago, she was shattered. But then she went back to school to become a teacher at the community center. And she says all the children in the neighborhood are now her children.

Shanti is surprised to see me arrive alone, since Faiza and I usually visit together. She's sitting in the small garden outside her home that's at the end of a lane. Shanti has planted tomatoes in tin cans, and they produce the juiciest fruit. I asked her once why they were so good, and she told me it's because she sings to them.

Now Shanti pats the space next to her and says, "Minni, come, come. So nice to see you."

Baba and Ma told me not to tell anyone that I witnessed water theft, so I of course keep quiet about that. But I show her the newspaper with the water mafia story.

She reads it and hands it back to me. "Ah yes, I know about these thieves. They steal water any way they can. They're especially busy when water's low in our lakes, like now, before monsoon season. Remember I told you that Mumbai is made of seven islands? Did you know we get our drinking water from seven sources?"

"I know the biggest lake is the Vihar, and near it is Tulsi Lake," I tell Shanti. "I'd love to visit them."

"So you shall someday," Shanti predicts. Then she counts on her fingers and names the five other lakes and reservoirs, and I repeat their names.

"All those lakes, and yet we still don't have enough fresh water. Too bad we can't drink the seawater," I say.

"Clever girl—that just might be in our future," Shanti says. "I heard the city approved a plan for a factory to take the salt out of the water."

"That will be real progress," I say. "Shanti, I've been thinking a lot about the story you told us about how the land here was reclaimed from the sea."

"What were you thinking?"

"You said the land was once marsh and that the ground wasn't as strong as we thought it was."

She raises her brows.

"My family wasn't as strong as I thought it was either. My mother's sick and had to go stay with her family in their village. Sanjay left too . . ." I can't trust myself to say anything more.

But even without more details, Shanti understands what I need to hear.

"Minni, I did say that the ground was marshy, but don't forget that it has held us up for centuries. It may not be the strongest, but it's stronger than you think."

I hadn't thought of it like that. Maybe I'm stronger than I think too—I did climb the ladder after all.

Then she gets up, gets a comb, and unbraids my messy hair. With Ma being sick, I had braided it myself and didn't do the best job. Without a word, Shanti untangles the knots just like Ma does.

Gradually, with each stroke of the comb, I relax.

Shanti holds my hand and tells me, "You're not alone, dear Minni. And you're very brave."

Over and over she chants it, like it's a mantra. "You're not alone. You're very brave."

And slowly I begin to believe her.

- 15 -

Ma has not been gone *that* long, yet it looks like a month's worth of dirty laundry has piled up. Both of my school uniforms need washing, and Baba is almost out of clean clothes. So on Saturday morning I get up early to tackle another task that Ma had somehow found time to do and that I took for granted.

Hauling extra water to the small tiled space behind our house that doubles as our place to wash ourselves is no easy chore. I remember seeing Ma beat our clothes and bedding against a washing stone to get them clean, so I mimic her. I'm soaking wet but still sweating by the time I hang the clothes on a line to dry.

When Baba comes home and sees the laundry drying in the breeze, he pats me on the head and smiles.

I'm trying to study and Baba's resting when his phone rings. Without a word, he hands it to me.

"Minni Meow," I hear Sanjay say. "Can you hear me?"

How did he know I needed to speak to him? I've missed him so much that I've been wearing his T-shirt to sleep, but I don't tell him that.

Instead I say, "I'm here—but not if you call me Minni Meow!" He laughs, and it feels good to squabble over my silly name. To remember a time when that felt important.

"I climbed up onto the roof all by myself," I brag.

He sputters. "No! You hate that creaky ladder. How did you become so adventurous?"

"Who knows," I tease him. "Maybe I'll start jumping from house to house like you and Amit."

"Minni, I said you're adventurous, not foolish," he says. "Remember what happened to Amit?"

"I was just joking," I say.

But Sanjay is not kidding when he says, "Remember—trouble can take a minute to get into and a lifetime to get out of."

"Now you sound just like Baba, Sanjay!" I say. And then I add, "Hopefully not a lifetime, just a few months."

"Don't hold your breath, Minni. I think I'm here for a while."

"Well then, at least you like it there."

"I do," Sanjay says. "If it weren't for missing you all, it'd be perfect."

"And Amit? How's he doing?"

"Not surprisingly, it turns out our Amit's a city boy. There's not much wheeling and dealing for him to do on the farm. And he misses the kids he rapped with."

"I stopped to listen to them a few days ago," I say. "They definitely need his skills. No one makes rhymes like Amit."

"That's for sure. He's trying to get a group together here. It's funny listening to them learning to keep the beat. But anyway, he really can't wait to get back to the neighborhood. Amit says he never wants to live anywhere else, even when he's a star."

"I'll be sure to remind him of that when he is a star," I say.

- 16 -

At the end of school I hurry to the bathroom and change out of my uniform skirt and blouse into a simple dress Ma made.

On any other day Faiza and I would walk home giggling. Today we hug goodbye instead, and I wonder if I'm saying goodbye not just to our routine, but to my childhood.

Today I will take the bus to Ma's job, which for the next month is my job. Faiza will walk home alone, or she might make new friends who have healthy mothers at home.

Seeing my gloomy face, Faiza hugs me again and whispers, "You'll be fine."

I walk toward the bus stop, clutching the fare in my sweaty hand.

The bus stops with a noisy grinding, whooshing sound, and I get in. Then I see Faiza racing toward the bus, yelling, "Wait! Wait for me."

The bus driver shakes his head but waits.

Faiza pays the small fare and clambers on. She sits by me. "What're you doing?" I ask. "Why are you riding the bus?"

"To be there for you," says Faiza. "If it weren't for you lecturing me, making me do homework, and sharing your notes, I wouldn't be in seventh grade. I would've left school last year."

I brave a smile. "Not true!"

"True!" she says.

The ride is short, and we scramble out of the bus. Ma said she often walks when the weather's not so hot.

We cross the street and head toward one of the high-rise buildings I've seen looming behind our neighborhood every day of my life. Across from the building is a beautiful flame tree with its branches reaching out. Faiza and I stand under it and look at the building with its gleaming paint and wraparound balconies. Ma thought I could manage her job, and I cling to her belief in me.

"I suppose it will be interesting to see the inside," I say to Faiza. "Maybe it'll be an adventure?"

She nods. "Yes! You never know."

The wrought-iron gates are closed, and a security guard asks, "Where are you going?"

"Anita Ma'am's h-h-house," I stutter.

"Are you Rohini's girl, Meena?" he asks.

I nod. So I will be Meena here.

Faiza squeezes my hand. "Minni, hold your head up. And remember this is only a temporary job—it's not forever."

"Thanks," I manage to say. Faiza has come as far as she can; she cannot go beyond this gate. I must go alone.

The security guard opens the gate. He walks with me to the lobby. The marble floor shines so bright I'm afraid I might slip.

"Meena," says the security guard as we step into the elevator. "Your ma is proud of you. She says you're as smart as her sister."

"She said that?" I say.

The ride comes to a bumpy halt. The guard slides the metal-latticed door and then pushes open the wooden outer door. I step out, and he leaves.

I'm absorbing what the guard just told me. Ma never told me that she thinks I'm as smart as her sister Meena. I always dream of making Ma proud, and knowing she already is makes me hold my head a little higher.

- 17 -

The hallway outside the apartment is lined with big, leafy plants in brass pots that shine and reflect my feet like a mirror. On the wall there's a painting of a blue horse tossing its mane. Gingerly I press the doorbell. Under my breath I count one hundred, two hundred, three hundred. Sanjay once told me counting helps him to stay calm. Maybe it'll do the same for me.

A lady wearing jeans and a loose blue tunic opens the door. She smiles. "You must be Rohini's daughter, Meena. Come in."

I nod. This is Anita Ma'am. The woman I have heard about for years. The woman who paid my school fee, and whose generosity my family depends on. Finally, I meet her. I hope she realizes that this is my first job and is kind.

I step into a new world.

It looks like something from the movies. The marble

floor sparkles beneath soft carpets. The furniture is cream-colored and looks unlived in. Shiny, jewel-colored pillows are arranged perfectly on the sofas. The coffee table in the center has a collection of silver bells and big books. Huge windows look out onto the city, and an ornate swing with brass chains hangs in front of one of them. I'd feel like a queen surveying her kingdom if I was ever lucky enough to sit in it.

Anita Ma'am is saying something to me, so I need to stop gawking. She wants me to follow her into the kitchen.

But it turns out the kitchen is full of stuff to gawk at too. There's the biggest, cleanest sink I've ever seen, with its own sparkling tap. Attached to it is a water filter like the ones I've seen in TV ads that promise to give you the cleanest, most refreshing water on earth. I can't wait to drink a glass and taste it.

Anita Ma'am shows me the areas of the apartment that I will be responsible for cleaning and points to a closet in the hallway with cleaning supplies.

We pass a closed door as we walk down the hall, and Anita Ma'am says, "You will not go in there. That's my mother-in-law's room. Perhaps you will meet her tomorrow." She rolls her eyes as she says this, and I don't understand why, but I remember Ma's instructions to not ask questions unless necessary.

Then she tells me she wants me to start by cleaning the bathroom in her daughter's room. I'm eager to see Pinky, the one who sent us the perfect mango and has curly hair that Ma combed. The one who Ma said is sweet. I hope so.

Pinky is lying on a pink rose-patterned bedspread on a big platform bed. She looks like a princess in a fairy tale. I can't help staring at her wall of filled bookshelves. Has she read all these books? Then I see a desk in the corner of the room, and it holds Pinky's very own computer. I'd like to reach out and touch everything. For a moment, a pang of jealousy stabs me. Does Pinky realize how lucky she is?

"Pinky, this is Rohini's daughter, Meena," Anita Ma'am says.

Pinky and I smile at each other.

Anita Ma'am leads me into a bathroom that's attached to Pinky's bedroom, and I stare at it in wonder.

In my neighborhood, thirty families share a bathroom at the end of our lane that has seven stalls. And for a bath or shower, most of us use a bucket of water.

Pinky has her very own tub. She can close her own door and bathe in it in privacy. Imagine.

"When you're done, come and find me," Anita Ma'am says, and then leaves.

Once she's gone, Pinky leaps off the bed and joins me. "Meena, how old are you?"

"I'm twelve."

"Me too!" says Pinky. Her curly dark hair is held back by a white headband and bounces around her face.

I stand in the doorway to the bathroom and look at the shiny marble floors and counters. I'm not sure what I need to clean, since it looks cleaner than any bathroom I've ever seen. Sometimes our neighborhood toilet makes me gag.

Pinky follows me into the bathroom. "I'm bored," she tells me. "Let me help you."

I have a feeling she's not supposed to do that, and I don't want to get in trouble. But when I object, she says, "Don't worry, Mom won't know, but I can just keep you company if you prefer."

Pinky watches as I sprinkle some cleaning powder and start to scrub. How long am I supposed to take? Ma gave me instructions for everything, and I wish I'd listened more carefully.

"You need to wet it first," says Pinky. "I've watched Rohini do it."

Why does Pinky call Ma by her name as if she is her equal? I'd never call someone my mother's age by her name. I always call them Aunty or Ma'am.

I look around the bathroom. There is no bucket filled with water.

Then Pinky turns on the tap, and to my astonishment, water gushes out. It flows freely in the middle of the day. Like it's magic.

The rich really do live in a different world!

I hear Anita Ma'am calling Pinky, and she runs off.

On my own, I stand at one end of the bathroom, and I walk across to the other end with deliberate steps. Like a girl on a tightrope.

I count my steps.

One, two, three, four, five, six, seven, eight, nine, ten.

Pinky's bathroom is as big as our house.

I do my best as I move from task to task, not sure if I am doing anything right, and finally I end up in the kitchen.

Anita Ma'am tells me that there is leftover dough in the refrigerator that Ma made. "It will be enough for six rotis. It's usually just me, my mother-in-law, and my daughter. My husband works most evenings."

She hovers over me as I prepare to make the rotis, which makes my hands turn clumsy. But when I begin to knead the dough, the movement calms my shaking hands.

Ma made this dough.

The thought comforts me. It feels like she's with me, helping me.

I make six balls and start to roll one. It sticks to the round wooden board. I forgot to flour the board.

I scrape up the dough and restart after pouring out the flour. But my second attempt is not much better. The roti looks like the map of India, so I start yet again.

Anita Ma'am shakes her head and leaves the kitchen. On her way out, she mumbles, "Rohini said she taught you to make rotis."

I feel my heart thumping. I cannot make a liar of my ma. I have to do better, or I'll lose this job on the first day.

I take several deep breaths. *Minni,* I hear Sanjay saying, *you can do anything you set your mind on.*

On my third try, I roll a circle. I cook it. My rotis are not as soft as Ma's, but they're okay. I'm sweating by the time I am done, as if the task required me to move a mountain.

THAT NIGHT I think about Pinky's beautiful bathroom as I wash up before bed. I write in my journal.

water flows through the taps in Pinky's bathroom.
The tap doesn't need a marigold garland wrapped
   around it.
Money, not prayers, makes the water flow.

- 18 -

The next day, I wake up with Baba. The sun is barely awake, but I'm a working girl now. "How was your first day?" he asks.

"I wasn't fired," I say.

He smiles. "Jai ho! Victory."

My parents have more faith in me than I do. They think I can hold this job. If only they knew how close I came to losing it on my very first day.

Baba watches me gather the containers for water. "Beti," he says, "I wish I could help. If only I could be in two places at a time. But now I must get to work even earlier."

"It's okay, Baba," I say. "But why?"

"Your mother would clean, peel, and chop the vegetables for the pakoda batter," he says. "Now I've got to do it myself."

How did Ma do so much each day? Did she have more than two hands? And how did she usually do it with a smile?

Now I understand why she often asked me to massage her

shoulders and Sanjay to massage her feet. And why on some days she'd get angry and yell at all of us. It wasn't very often, but Sanjay and I knew not to upset her on those days.

The sun has risen by the time I go outside to the tap. It doesn't gush like it did in Pinky's bathroom, but the stream is steady. My mind wanders to yesterday as I wait for the containers to fill.

Last night I just served dinner to Pinky and her mother. Her grandmother didn't come to the table. Lata, Anita Ma'am's personal maid and family cook, took a plate to the grandmother's room. Unlike me, Lata lives with the family. I cannot imagine that. I counted the hours until I could leave and go back to my world. Lata said she came to live and work for Pinky's family when she was thirteen. I really can't imagine that!

Nobody ever asked me to eat. I served the rotis I'd made along with a delicious-smelling dish of palak paneer made by Lata. I would have loved a bite.

I returned home exhausted to an empty house. Ma always had food waiting for us, but now I'd have to figure out meals myself.

I found some biscuits and sat on the stoop. I was sharing one with Moti when Naan Aunty came by and asked, "Is that your dinner?"

I nodded. The sweet biscuits were making me feel better.

"I'll be right back," she said.

She returned a few minutes later with a naan and a bowl

of cauliflower sabzi. Each bite melted in my mouth and filled a huge hole inside me.

"I will bring you some food tomorrow while you are getting used to your new routine," she said.

When I thanked her, she told me, "Your ma has helped me stand when I faltered. In this neighborhood we are here for each other."

ALL OF A sudden, the sound of the water filling my bucket interrupts my thoughts. I need to get moving.

I boil the water while I get ready for school. Ma isn't here to braid my hair, so I just collect it all into a ponytail.

By the time I've finished boiling and straining all the water, I realize there's no time to make breakfast, so I grab a banana and a piece of bread and rush out the door.

I sprint to the main street not expecting to see Faiza, but there she is, standing there like a gift from the world.

"We should run," she says.

We fly as fast as our feet allow and get to school gasping for breath. But the final bell has rung, and the main door is closed.

I look down at myself. My skirt's wrinkled. My blouse has escaped the waistband. And my ponytail's coming loose.

I tuck my blouse in and try to smooth my skirt.

Seeing Faiza's hair in neat braids and her ironed uniform

makes me miss my ma even more. I guess I need to do a better job at growing up.

Shiva, the school guard, sits in his chair and looks at us. "You know the rules," he says.

"We do, we do," says Faiza. "We're never late, so just today, please, can you let us in?"

I keep staring at the guard's face because he looks familiar. When he twirls his mustache, it comes to me.

"You drink tea at my baba's tea stall," I blurt out.

"The tea stall by the main road?" he asks.

I nod. "Yes, that's the one! The Jai Ho tea stall."

"Your baba makes the best pakodas," he says. "Why are you late? Slept too long?"

If only. The days when I didn't wake up and Ma and Sanjay had to shake me awake feel like a distant dream. Ma would wait on me like I was princess. She'd roll a roti smeared with jam for me to eat on the way.

I tell him that my ma had to go to the village because she's been ill.

"Why are you late?" he asks Faiza.

"I waited for Minni," she says.

He shakes his head at both of us but goes to the door and peeks in, signaling for us to wait. When the coast is clear, he lets us sneak in. We enter the classroom from the back door. Miss Shah sees us but, thankfully, doesn't say a word.

When we're seated, Faiza passes a note.

Minni, Ammi has packed enough lunch for both of us. She made your favorite, jeera aloo.

I read it a few times.

Her mother remembered that I love jeera aloo and that Ma wasn't there to pack me lunch, so she did. Naan Aunty brought me dinner. Faiza waited for me, and Shiva the guard let us in. Miss Shah didn't question us for being late.

At lunch I feel the caring in every bite. Shanti told me I wasn't alone, and now I see what she meant.

This growing-up thing is hard—and the carefree days of my childhood may never return. But I have so many people here to help.

That night I write in my journal:

Your family is always part of you,
in your blood and in your memories.
Your true friends are with you too.
They hold you in their hearts and walk beside you.
So that even the days you walk by yourself,
    you're not alone.

When I arrive at work, Pinky opens the door all excited.

"Meena," she says. "Mom is going out today."

Anita Ma'am is all dressed up and smells like a jasmine garden. Her chiffon sari looks like a pink cloud, and she has on pretty dangling earrings. "Meena," she says, "no cleaning today—Pinky has begged me to let you play with her. All I need you to do is just make some rotis, then you are free."

I'm surprised that Pinky is so eager to hang out with me.

After her mother leaves, Pinky follows me to the kitchen and watches as I make the dough. "You're so clever," she says. "I would have no idea how to make dough or rotis."

I don't tell her that I didn't either till a few weeks ago.

"But, Meena," she says, "can you try to make your rotis thinner and softer, like your mother's? My grandmother said she couldn't eat them yesterday."

I nod. I'm glad Pinky is telling me the truth.

"I want you to stay," she says. "I like having you here."

"Thanks, Pinky." I smile at her and say, "But you must have lots and lots of friends. You don't need me."

Pinky bites her nails just like I've started doing recently. "I don't. Because I'm not allowed to go *anywhere* on my own. Not even to play with the other kids who live in this building."

"Why?" I ask, surprised.

"My parents want to keep me safe," she says.

I don't understand why Pinky would be in danger in her own apartment building, and I feel bad that she's not allowed to go out on her own. She has so much and so little. She's like a princess locked in a tower.

When I'm done, she claps. "Now we can play." Pinky gets us a bowl of potato chips, and we go to her room, where she teaches me the rules to a new card game that she got from a relative in America. Soon we're laughing and bargaining.

Pinky wins the first game. I win the second game.

"Uno," I shout.

When I win the third game, she tosses a pillow at me, and I toss it back.

She is hiding cards behind her back and I'm wrestling with her, trying to get them, when the door opens. An older lady with white hair in a bun, wearing a white tunic and loose salwar pants, steps in. She looks like she has eaten a sour pickle.

"Pinky," she says. Her voice is like the edge of a steel knife.

"Grandmother." Pinky jumps up, and the bowl of chips topples over as her hand of cards scatters onto the floor.

I jump to my feet too.

"You," she orders, lifting her chin and waving her hand as if she's swatting a fly. "Go to the kitchen."

Pinky looks scared. I walk out as fast as I can.

I retreat into the kitchen, but Pinky's grandmother's words follow me like a swarm of stinging bees. She knows that I can hear and obviously doesn't care.

"What're you doing with the servant girl?" she shouts.

"Just playing cards," Pinky says. "Mom knows, and it's okay. She's my friend."

"Friend?" she repeats. "Do you even know where these low-caste people live? Do you know the kind of germs that breed in those slums? You don't know—she might have TB."

There is silence. Pinky has decided not to say anything.

"Pinky, you need to grow up. Don't be a stupid girl," her grandmother says. "You know Rohini lied when she said the girl is trained. She cannot even roll a roti. They're all liars."

Then I hear her grandmother's footsteps going back down the hall. Her door slams shut.

I pick up the broom and start sweeping with hard strokes, wishing the floor was the awful grandmother.

Ma taught me the rules. I'm not allowed to have any feelings or thoughts. I should never forget my place. I forgot that Pinky was my employer's daughter.

After a while, a puffy-eyed Pinky finds me mopping the floor.

"Meena," she says, "I'm sorry about that. Let's go back and play in my room. I can lock my door."

I think about her offer. Her grandmother told her to grow up, and my mother told me the same thing. But it means very different things for each of us.

My voice is tired when I say, "I don't think it's a good idea right now. I'm not really your friend, Pinky. I'm the help. No matter what we pretend."

Pinky's face crumples just like mine did when I heard her grandmother's words.

ON MY WAY home, I stop at Baba's tea stall. Ma might not approve of me eating just fried pakodas for dinner, but she would understand me wanting to see Baba. The sun is setting, and the lights strung on the tea stall shine.

Baba lifts the kettle and pours tea into the small cups from a height with a flourish. He says the pouring is important to how it tastes and it makes the liquid foam. His customers watch with awe.

"Minni," says one the customers, "how you've grown! I haven't seen you in months."

"Minni is doing Rohini's job and going to school," Baba says with pride.

I blush. I'm glad he's been too busy to ask me how the job is going.

"We know you are a smart girl. How are your studies?" asks an aunty.

Hari Chacha, who has worked for my father for years, walks by and answers, "School comes easy for our Minni. She's a whiz kid!"

I laugh. "Not always. But it's going pretty well. My teacher, Miss Shah, is so nice and clever."

I take a breath. They're listening, so I continue. "And you know Faiza, right? She's in my class this year and sits across from me. We're so lucky, we get to walk to school and be together most of the day."

Aunty pats me on my back. "It's good to have a best friend like that."

The biscuits dunked in the hot sweet tea melt in my mouth and fill my empty stomach. But the affection surrounding me fills me even more. This is just where I needed to be this evening, in a friendly place and with people who care—people who don't think I'm less than them.

- 20 -

On Sunday morning, I do my water chores at dawn. It feels like I've been working without a pause since Ma left. I am happy to be able to sit for a moment and breathe.

It was Shanti who taught us how to breathe during one of her story times. She made us all sit with straight spines and put one hand on our bellies, just below the ribs, and the other hand on our chests.

"Take a breath through your nose, and let your belly push your hand out," Shanti instructed us.

One of the uncles who had a big belly burst out laughing. With each deep breath, he wiggled his tummy and had us all giggling, including Shanti.

Then she said, "Breathe out through your lips as if you're whistling."

Of course, that led to the whistling of songs.

So much has happened since then, but Shanti's breathing

lessons have taught me to keep inhaling through it all. One day at a time, one breath at a time.

Then I hear my name called, and it sounds like Shanti. Did I make her appear by thinking of her? She has never come to my house. We always meet under the banyan tree or at her home.

The voice gets louder, more urgent. "Minni!"

I rush outside. Shanti strides up and pumps her fist into the air. "You got the scholarship, Minni! You got it."

I'm puzzled. What scholarship? I never applied for one.

Shanti explains, "The scholarship for the computer class. There was a raffle, and your ma must have entered your name."

Then I recall Ma mentioning the class that day we ate the mango. She was going to find out more details, but obviously she did more than that! Ma may be far away, but she's still with me. Watching over me yet again.

"How did you find out?" I ask.

"Because I volunteer at the community center," Shanti says.

Of course she does. Shanti helps everywhere.

Shanti's loud excitement has attracted Naan Aunty and a few others. Even Moti joins us and barks in excitement.

Good news spreads fast in our neighborhood, trickling like water into the smallest crack—we are so thirsty for it.

It only takes a minute for the news to reach Faiza.

She runs up screaming, her hands outstretched, with one braid done and the other half of her hair flying loose.

"Minni!" She hugs me, and we jump in place.

Shanti sits on my stoop. Moti lies by her side, and just like that, it's story time.

"Once upon a time," says Shanti, "there lived a girl, in our neighborhood, in a city that once was seven islands, who dreamed big dreams and was very lucky."

Everyone smiles and looks at me. For a moment I forget that I'm a low-caste girl from a poor neighborhood. I am that lucky girl instead.

"Her dreams were as tall as the sea link bridge and as deep as the ocean. Like the sea link, they connected her present and her future," she says.

Naan Aunty sighs.

Faiza hugs herself.

Shanti can spin a story from breaths of air.

"Shanti," I ask through the glow of being the hero of my own story, "what do I do to sign up for this class?"

"Goodness me!" she says. "It's why I came. You need to go and accept the scholarship and attend an introduction at noon."

It's barely ten A.M., so I have plenty of time.

"Shanti, when is the class? I've got school and a job."

"Oh, don't worry," she says. "It's on Sunday mornings."

The worry floats away. But then I wonder—is this too good to be true?

FAIZA AND I go by the tea stall to tell Baba the news.

"Jai ho!" he shouts when I tell him, pointing to the sign on the stall. "Everyone, listen, listen. Good news!"

Faiza hops around and yells, "Minni got into a computer class."

Everyone turns and claps. Some echo Baba's "jai ho!"

Hari Chacha stops cleaning tables to pat me on my back.

Everyone wants to know more about the class and how I got in.

"It's because of Ma," I say. "She entered my name for the class."

Baba hands me his phone. "Call your ma—she will be so excited!"

We stand by the side of the stall, and I dial Ma's sister's number, hoping that she answers.

She does and immediately puts Ma on.

"Ma," I yell, "I got the scholarship. I got it."

There's silence.

"Minni?" she says. "Is that you?"

"Yes, Ma," I say. "I got the scholarship to the computer class. I'm going for the introduction class today. Did you put in my name? You didn't tell me."

"Minni," Ma says, "I enter your name and Sanjay's to win so many things. Bicycles, books, toys, shoes, a shopping trip for Diwali. I've been doing it since you were little."

"Oh, Ma," I say. "You never told me."

Ma laughs. "Because there was nothing to tell. We never ever won anything before."

"But we *did* this time, Ma," I say. "We sure did!"

- 21 -

Before class, I change into the dress that Ma made for me last year. She found the fabric in a sale bin, and the purple curlicue pattern on it looks like a henna design.

I skip over to the class. The sky is bright blue, and I spy roses blooming in a window pot. For some reason it's not as hot today.

Everything feels festive—even the red and blue, yellow and green saris drying on the clotheslines feel like decorations flapping in the wind, celebrating my good luck.

"I'm Priya," the computer teacher introduces herself. She looks Indian, but she speaks with an accent I've never heard before, which we learn is American. Priya has come to India to teach and work for a year.

When we call her Priya Ma'am, she says, "No! No! Please don't call me Ma'am. Call me Priya."

Shanti, who is the volunteer helper, brings out her trusty

conch shell to grab our attention. She wags her finger and says, "No, that would be rude."

Priya Ma'am turns bright red. "I'm so sorry. I didn't mean to be disrespectful."

Shanti then suggests, "They could call you Priya Didi. *Didi* means 'big sister.'"

Priya is thrilled. "I'd love that. I always wanted some little sisters."

"Well, now you have ten, lucky lady!" Shanti says, and we all laugh.

Then we turn to the computers. Shanti tells us a large business donated them.

I was so dazzled by our new teacher when I came in that I didn't pay attention to all the computers sitting on desks. The screens glow like fully lit moons, and each one has a picture of a bird gliding over a mountain with its wings outstretched.

Priya Didi looks at all of us and says, "That is called a screen saver. I chose an eagle. I imagine that this class will teach you girls to fly."

She explains that we will be learning an exciting new language in this class—just like Hindi or English or Marathi. We'll discover secret codes that she will teach us to understand.

But before we all take our seats, she has us sit in a circle on the floor and says she wants to get to know us. She asks why we came to the class and about our families. No teacher has ever asked us such things before. When I attended the free government school in first and second grade, there were almost seventy kids in a class. In my class now, we have fifty kids. Miss Shah couldn't speak to each of us even if she wanted to.

After a minute of silent surprise, we all start talking at once.

Priya Didi claps like a child.

"Let's start with you," she says, pointing to a girl sitting by me. "Then we'll go clockwise."

I'll be the last to speak.

They say their families said computers were too hard to learn, but they wanted to prove them wrong.

They say they saved a rupee a day for a year.

A girl about my age named Gita says she was told that computers were not for her, but she came anyway.

Another says her father and mother said computers were the future, so she had to learn.

Some girls say they've never touched a computer but can't wait.

Amina, the girl sitting next to me, speaks softly. She says she knows a person who learned to code and got a job in an office with air-conditioning, and maybe she can too someday.

When it's my turn, I say my ma entered my name in the raffle, and today I feel like the luckiest girl on earth.

Then Priya Didi teaches us how to start the computer,

how to use the mouse, and how to move the cursor across the screen. The clacking of the keys sounds like music. It feels like I've stepped through a magical door.

But it is confusing too—there is so much to learn.

I curl my hand over the mouse, and an arrow dances all over the screen.

Gita is watching over my shoulder. "Minni," she says, "we have to click the button on the mouse to make that arrow stop on something."

"What if we mess it up?" I whisper to Gita.

"Then the mouse will come to life and bite you," Gita jokes.

Priya Didi walks by and tells us she's happy to see we are getting comfortable with our computers. "And don't worry," she says, "the computer won't break."

It's good to hear that. I remember the two computers in our school. Miss Shah once took us to the computer room, but the principal told us, "Look, don't touch. Too many fingers and too few keyboards."

I wanted to ask what they were there for if we weren't allowed to use them, but didn't. I didn't want it to reflect badly on Miss Shah.

Time tricks us in this class. The two hours feel like two minutes. Before we all leave, Priya Didi shares chocolates with us that she brought from America that are deliciously sweet and gooey.

While we snack on them, she says, "Speaking of learning new languages, I need help improving my Hindi. Will my little sisters teach me?"

We all yell, "Yes!"

We teach her the Hindi word for "today," *aaj*.

"How do you say 'tomorrow' in Hindi?" Priya Didi asks.

"Aane wala kal," I say.

"Once you girls learn the language of computers, you will be ready for tomorrow, for the future," she says.

It feels like the clouds part in the sky and the sun peeps out when she says that.

I walk outside with Gita, and as we part, she says, "See you next week. I wish we could come back sooner. I can't wait to learn more."

"Me too," I say, smiling. "Watch out, future—here we come!"

I still feel giddy with excitement when I get home, so I take out my notebook, and inspiration strikes.

This brand-new language
has fascinating words.
Apps and algorithms,
bits and bytes,
cookies and clips,
data and disks,
windows, rooms, and firewalls,

home pages, mirrors,
monitors, and mouse.
Where will it take me?
To college? To a computer job?
This brand-new language
has new words for all my new dreams.

The intense heat is back on Monday, and I decide to take the bus to work after school. As we roll away, I look out the window and see Faiza with some other girls from our neighborhood. They are standing in front of a market, laughing and looking at a magazine, and sharing a package of chips. I would give a lot to be with them right now, rather than headed to a job that I don't like and am no good at. I know Faiza will always be my best friend, but I imagine her moving on and me being left behind. I wonder if I need to find new friends who also have jobs. Except where is the time for friends?

When I arrive at the high-rise, I'm surprised to see Pinky open the door.

"I'm so glad to see you," she says. "I was scared you wouldn't come."

Why wouldn't I come? Did she think her grandmother's

words would keep me away? If only I could explain to Pinky that jagged words are flung at people like me all the time. I was taught to swallow my pride and sweep them away. I don't have the choice to leave or act hurt.

I now have a routine at work. I dust and sweep and mop the apartment. Then I knead the dough and roll rotis. On days that Anita Ma'am doesn't have her yoga class, she often follows me around from room to room, making sure that I've not missed a speck of dust and pointing out barely visible blemishes on her shining white marble floors.

I want to tell her that she could use her eagle-eye vision to do something more useful, but I bite my tongue.

Instead, I say, "Yes, ma'am."

I'm changing the sheets on Pinky's bed when Pinky's grandmother enters. "Meena," she says. "Did you wash your hands before you touched the clean sheets?"

"Yes, ma'am," I say. I remember one of Ma's lessons. Do as you're told. Don't question.

As she leaves, she says, "Pinky, don't close your door."

"Yes, Grandmother," Pinky calls out.

Why is Pinky's grandmother keeping an eye on us? What does she imagine will happen?

Pinky whispers, "Did you like that card game?"

When I'm silent, she says, "I had so much fun."

I did have fun. I remember Pinky gave my ma the mango. I remember Ma telling me that she was a nice girl. She can be nice, but I'm exhausted. Everything feels like a minefield here.

"I liked the card game," I say.

"Meena," she says. "Can I call you Minni? I heard your mom call you that."

I want to say, *My friends call me Minni too, but you're not my friend. If you were my friend, you would say, "Minni, my grandmother is wrong about you."*

Instead I say, "Sorry, but I have to get to work."

I stretch the sheets, tuck the corners tight, and keep my mouth shut.

ON THE WALK home, I imagine Ma or Sanjay being home, waiting for me. I decide I will never take that for granted again when it actually happens.

When I get home, I see the next-best thing: Faiza is waiting for me on my stoop.

I can feel my tense, rigid shoulders fall back into place. My brow relaxes. I am no longer in the wrong world.

"I thought you might need some cheering up," Faiza says. "Ma made kebabs. We saved a few for you."

I reach for the food and, without a word, take a bite.

"Ooh!" I say. "You have no idea how good that tastes."

"I do, actually." Faiza grins. "I just had them for dinner."

She waits patiently for me to finish eating and then says,

"So now tell me what's going on with the evil grandmother. How has she insulted you lately?"

"Oh, Faiza, she's just the worst! The other day she told Pinky I might carry diseases, being so low caste and all."

"Pinky's grandmother is a lowly human being, Minni. If I ever see her, I will punch her"—Faiza's fist hits the air—"for you."

"Thank you, Faiza. You are too kind," I say, and burst out laughing.

I decide that the next time Pinky's grandmother insults me, I'll cheer myself up by imagining Faiza having a movie-style fight with her.

- 23 -

On Sunday afternoon, Faiza and I take a walk in the neighborhood, and Moti follows us. Faiza has brought Moti a bone.

"Are you trying to bribe him?" I ask.

Moti crunches it in minutes and stays close to Faiza afterward.

"Moti loves me more," says Faiza.

"Traitor," I say to Moti.

As we walk around, I notice things that I didn't think much about before working at the high-rise. First of all, our streets are barely streets—they're more like alleys—and the deeper you go into our neighborhood, the narrower they become. Our electric lines are not in neat rows; instead, huge clumps of them hang over houses. But worst of all—we don't have swept sidewalks, and there are piles of trash everywhere. And while some of the smells on the street are good, a lot are *not*. But we take pride in keeping ourselves neat and clean, and I know a bunch of people have started a movement to clean up our streets.

I wish our neighborhood was tidier right now, but none of this makes *us* any different. We work as hard as anybody in that other world, and so many people I know have their own businesses, making clothes or food or doing laundry or recycling.

And maybe we even have more fun when we play games and sing and rap and dance our hearts out.

Sunday is my favorite day because everyone has a little time for fun. One of the kids playing cricket on our lane whacks the ball and scores a four. Everyone cheers, and the boy beams with pride.

The women gathered under the banyan tree where Shanti tells stories look like they are enjoying themselves as they gossip and shell peas.

At the end of our street, one of the uncles has run an extension cord and placed the TV outside his house for everyone to watch. *Gully Boy* plays on the screen. Ranveer Singh is rapping. The houses and neighborhood look like mine in this movie, which is rare. Most Bollywood films are shot in homes that look like Pinky's.

Faiza and I loop back to my house and sit on the stoop. I tell Faiza about Priya Didi and learning to code and that we'll learn to build apps. I've missed sharing everything that happens to me with Faiza, so I paint every detail, including what Priya Didi wears and how she always drinks water from a tin water bottle.

Then Faiza surprises me. "Do you think you could talk about something other than Priya Didi all the time?"

"What? I don't talk about her all the time."

Faiza rolls her eyes.

"I'm sorry if I do, but if you met her, you'd know why," I tell Faiza. "She's like a really cool big sister and talks to us like we're her equals."

"That's nice," she says. "But between your job and Pinky and her horrible grandmother, and now Priya Didi, you never ask me how I am."

I'm lost for words.

"App, snap, what is that?" she says.

I start to explain, and Faiza waves me away. "I'm kidding—I don't want to know."

The sounds of crows cawing at sunset and honking cars fill the silence. But I don't know what to say to fill this new gap between me and Faiza. My life and hers were alike. Then my life changed so much, I can barely recognize it. I was worried that if I didn't tell her things, soon she wouldn't know me. But I forgot to ask Faiza about her life. I guess I assumed that because her life isn't upside down like mine, she wouldn't have things to share.

So now I ask, "Faiza, have you learned any new dance steps?"

"Why, yes, yes, I have," she says. "And I was chosen to be in a performance. But right now, we should probably be focused on exams. I'm terrified I might fail tomorrow. Do you have an app to fix that?"

"Wait, what are you talking about?" I say. "The exam is still two weeks away."

Faiza looks at me like I've lost my mind.

Then she gets up and shakes my shoulders.

"Minni, the exam might be two weeks away, but the practice test is tomorrow. Remember—it's the review packet test? Miss Shah told us the other day that if we do well, she'll give us bonus points on the real exam."

"What?" I say. "When did she tell us that?"

"On Monday," Faiza says. "She wrote it on the blackboard."

Monday? That must have been another one of the days I was late. Thank goodness I have Shiva secretly letting me in. He's had to about three or four times now. After that first day, he said he could only slip one of us in, not both. Faiza needs to be on time—but we would have figured that out anyway. One of us has to keep up.

I slump down.

The look on Faiza's face says she is realizing what happened too. "Then Miss Shah erased the board and started to write the important dates for Indian independence."

"I must have gotten in after she erased the board," I say. "Faiza, what're we going to do? I'm not ready for a test tomorrow!"

"But you're so smart, Minni! You know a lot of this stuff by heart," she says. "Me, though, I need all the help I can get, so let me run and get my books, and we'll study."

When Faiza returns, we start studying. She's right that I know a lot of the material well, but smaller details and dates of events can get jumbled in my stressed mind. The sun sinks. The lights on the sea link come on. We memorize. We read. We test each other. I help Faiza with the speed and distance problems.

Finally, near midnight, Faiza's older brother comes to walk her home.

I climb into my loft space and fall into bed, but I'm almost too exhausted to sleep.

Faiza was right. The computer class opened a door into a fairy-tale world, and I forgot my reality, which is far from magical.

- 24 -

I wake up the morning of the test with my brain in a fog after barely sleeping all week.

The sun rising over the horizon, splashing brilliant patches of yellow and red, doesn't cheer me as it typically does. Water still has to be collected, exam or no exam. I haul it in and set it to boil on the stove, keeping an eye on the time. I can't afford to be late today.

Faiza and I meet on the main road.

"Which year did Gandhiji lead the Salt March?" Faiza asks.

Seeing the fear in my eyes, Faiza says, "Don't worry. That may not be on the test anyway. There are so many other important facts."

I nod and force myself to take a bite of a biscuit I grabbed for breakfast on my way out.

As we're entering the class, Faiza whispers, "1930."

"What?" I say.

"The Salt March," she says.

"Quiet! No more talking," Miss Shah says, and distributes the test.

I've never been a last-minute learner or someone who can cram facts. I'm grabbed by a fear that I won't recall anything I learned last night.

I remember to inhale and exhale like Shanti taught me, and as the letters on the test paper settle down, I feel a strange calm. I read the first question. It's about the shortest distance between point A and point B. Good! I know this one.

Very soon, though, I get to a section on history that is full of dates and facts that I've not studied. I look over at Faiza. She's wiping her brow with her handkerchief. My brow is beaded with sweat too, and not just because of the heat.

After the class I linger till the others leave. I need to explain to Miss Shah. I can't have her think that I didn't bother to study for no reason. I tell her about Ma and the job and the water lines.

"You're doing a lot, Minni," Miss Shah says. "It's not surprising you can't focus on your work."

My stomach rumbles, and I realize I haven't eaten anything except a biscuit for breakfast and one for last night's dinner. I'm so embarrassed.

Miss Shah opens her bag and hands me a sandwich. "It's cheese and chutney," she says. "I'd like you to have it."

Gratefully, I take it.

"I'll grade your test tonight. So you'll know," Miss Shah promises.

I don't really need her to—I'm pretty sure I already know the result.

I've failed.

- 25 -

As I walk to work, I drag the words *Fail*, *Failed*, *Failure* like a weight around my ankles.

The minute I'm inside Anita Ma'am's house, she says, "Meena, make me a cup of tea, please. I'm so tired after shopping all day. Oh, and put all these bags in my room first."

She doesn't even blink at my tired, defeated face.

Fancy jewel-colored shopping bags sit by the couch. They even smell nice. I see silk saris sticking out of one of them.

"Yes, ma'am," I say.

Anita Ma'am's room feels like a refrigerator with its air-conditioning turned up. I place the bags at the foot of her bed. On a table by her bed, I see a picture. Anita Ma'am looks very young, and the man with her must be Pinky's father. It's odd, but I feel like I've seen him before.

Anita Ma'am enters and flops down on her bed.

"Meena," she says, "after you make my tea, will you make

some noodles for Pinky? Her exam's in two weeks, and she needs her strength to study."

"Yes, ma'am," I say.

I wonder if Anita Ma'am remembers that I go to school too. That I need to eat and study. Maybe she thinks I'm a robot who lives to serve?

As I make Pinky's snack—the same masala-flavored two-minute noodles I love—Ma's absence feels like a physical pain. If she were here, she would care that my exams were also two weeks away and make *me* noodles.

WHEN I TAKE the steaming bowl to her room, Pinky is at her desk working on her computer.

"Thank you, Meena," she says as I set the bowl down beside her.

I nod. No one else in this household has ever thanked me. She rolls a noodle onto her fork.

"This is a big bowl. Will you have some?" Pinky asks.

I would love to, but I know better, so I tell her no thanks.

"Meena," she says, "sometimes you look so sad. You must miss your mom so much."

"I do miss her a lot," I tell her. "It's quiet without her. And I don't see my father very often either. He works long hours."

"That must be hard. My father works all the time too," says Pinky. "He says he has more business than he can handle these days."

Pinky's father must be an important man to provide an apartment like this. With cars and marble floors, jewels and computers in every room.

"No wonder I've never seen him," I say. "Just a picture of him in your parents' room."

"That's from a long time ago—and I think it's the only picture of him in the house because Dad doesn't like photos," Pinky says. "He got injured at work a few years ago and hurt his face."

"I wish I had a photo of my ma," I tell Pinky. "I feel bad that I can't even remember how many days she's been gone."

"I miss your mom too. Nobody brushes my hair as gently as her," Pinky says, and we both smile thinking of Ma. Then she adds, "I like your long ponytail."

"You do?" I ask. "Ma used to braid it. I'm only wearing it this way because I don't have the time to do anything else, between school and work and my own family chores."

"I don't know how you do it, Meena . . . ," Pinky says, and then she looks embarrassed. "I'm sorry you have to work so hard. I can barely manage just my studies. I need to learn all the dates on this paper, ugh."

I look at the paper she's holding and see they're the dates that Faiza and I were memorizing about the Indian independence movement. "I need to learn those too. Want to quiz each other?"

"That would be great—but only if you share these noodles with me," Pinky says. "My grandmother isn't home."

I run to the kitchen and get another bowl.

Pinky splits the noodles, and we both slurp happily together.

If I had met Pinky at school, we'd probably be friends.

Except in our world, Pinky and I could *never* be in the same school.

- 26 -

I'M greeted at the entrance to school by Shiva, who refuses to meet my gaze. Normally he greets me with a broad grin and asks about my father, so it's very odd, especially since I'm not even late today.

I climb the worn steps hesitantly, and when Shiva opens the door, I'm greeted by the principal. She's wearing a white sari so starched that it barely moves. She looks almost like a statue. Her hands are crossed at her waist. My stomach clenches.

"Meena." She crooks her finger. "Come to my office. You too, Shiva."

Of course, being called to the principal's office is never good. In our school it only happens if you're in serious trouble.

As I step into the room, I feel like a fly stepping into a spider's web.

The principal's glass-topped desk holds only a small vase of flowers and her nameplate. She sits at her desk, and Shiva and I stand there, not knowing what to do and too afraid to ask. So, the principal is intimidating even to adults.

Ma once met her and said "that lady" peered into her soul and knew that she had dropped out of school and was uneducated. At the time we all thought it was funny, but maybe Ma was right.

The swinging door to the office creaks open, and Miss Shah steps in to join us.

Finally, the principal speaks. "I've been talking to some of the students in your class, Miss Shah, and they tell me that Meena often comes in late. You haven't been trying to hide things from me, have you?"

"Ma'am, there are circumstances you should know about," Miss Shah explains. "Minni's mother is ill and had to go stay with her family. So now Minni is not only doing all the household chores, she's filling in at her mother's job as a maid. All while studying and attending school."

The principal turns to me. "Is that true?"

I nod.

"Well, Meena, I am sorry to hear about your mother," the principal says. "I do hope she gets better soon."

Her words make me breathe a sigh of relief. She understands!

"Ma'am, I'm sorry too," Miss Shah says. "Minni is a good, hardworking student. I was trying to help her."

"That might be the case, Miss Shah, but it's hardly fair to

the other students for one of them to be allowed in late." At this, she eyes Shiva, and he mumbles his apologies too.

"To say nothing of the disruption your student is causing by her lateness. So are we all clear that this cannot continue? Meena, you will be on time, or you will not be here at all, you understand?"

Like Anita Ma'am, she doesn't expect an answer. She stands up quickly to dismiss us all, and her starched sari makes a crunching noise.

So much for sympathy.

- 27 -

Six A.M.

The stream of water sputters,
spits, gasps.
The water trickles,
brown, muddy,
drip, drip, drip, drip,
drip, drip, drip,
drip, drip,
drip.
The bucket is three-quarters empty.
The marigold garland draped around the tap
   is withered.
It doesn't matter.
I'm already late.
The water can take all day now.
what is going to become of me?

- 28 -

Mumbai's last two monsoon seasons didn't bring enough rain, so at this time of year—a few months before the next monsoon—the water levels in the lakes that supply the city have fallen below acceptable levels. Now the water supply to the rich residents of the city is reduced too. Even Anita Ma'am had her maid Lata hoard water in the tubs in case they run out later in the day. I heard her talking to some of the neighbors in the building about buying a water tank if the situation gets worse.

The municipality has asked all residents to conserve water. But how can we conserve the little we have? We don't waste a drop anyway.

Shanti told us that our parts of the city—the parts that people call the slums—get only 5 percent of the city's water supply, but we have almost 40 percent of Mumbai's population.

How does that add up? I asked her.

Shanti laughed and said, "Math won't supply this answer."

Now it's past seven thirty A.M., and the lines are barely moving with the water pressure being so low. These days, without Ma and Sanjay, I only have half the containers to fill, so in theory getting water should take less time. But math isn't going to supply this answer either.

I'm running so late, which means I'll miss a day of school— but maybe that's just as well, as there's a science test I know I'd fail.

Faiza will be arriving at school now. Yesterday she came over when I got home from work with her notes for the test.

"Here you go," she said, putting some papers in my hand. "You may not be in school, but I am. And, Minni, look at my notes—I didn't even erase!"

I nodded, overwhelmed by her kindness. But when I started to read her notes last night, I couldn't figure them out. I'd missed a bunch of classes that covered this material, and without having Miss Shah to explain it, the notes made no sense.

The sound of loud voices brings me back to the present. Apparently there's a water tap down the lane that seems to mysteriously have water. We all grab our buckets and pots and pans and sprint to the next line.

About a dozen women are already in front of me. One of them turns to me. "What're you doing at home, Minni?"

Before I can answer, another aunty says, "Rohini went to

her village. She's not well. Minni, have you had to stop going to school?"

It's funny how they ask me questions but don't wait for me to reply.

"Nothing wrong with that. I stopped in seventh grade too."

"At sixteen, you can be married, with that beautiful skin of yours."

"Men don't want to marry girls who are too educated, anyway."

"That is the truth."

I want to flee, but I need water.

"Rohini says you never stop talking. Where's that tongue of yours today?" one asks.

My brother's friend Latika arrives and overhears the conversation. She places her hand on my shoulder in support. She and I both know that the aunties are not thinking of how their words might affect me. And that anything I say will be misunderstood anyway.

"But our Minni is a smart one. She does well in school."

"Hope she doesn't think she's smarter than us. Don't you be getting too good for us with all your education, Minni."

"Look at Latika—she sells magazines by the traffic lights, helps her family, makes a living. That's a respectful daughter."

They're like vultures, and I'm the carcass. Latika looks at my crumpled face and whispers, "They don't realize what they're saying. Try to ignore them."

I do try, but it's hard. Finally, it's my turn. Mercifully, I am able to fill my two buckets fast.

Latika is next.

I wait for her, and when she's done, she smiles at me and we walk away together.

The women laugh as if it's a big joke.

"They're just bored and a little jealous," Latika says. "I'm sorry about your mom and that you had to miss school today. Do you want to come work with me? My partner can't make it."

I look at her eager face.

There's no reason I can't go with her, so I say yes.

- 29 -

Latika hands me a stack of magazines. We are positioned at the bottom of the overpass, where cars must come to a halt after leaving the highway. I'm supposed to rush over and sell magazines before the traffic light turns green, which is only a few minutes.

I approach the cars, and not one person buys a magazine. They keep their windows rolled up and wave me away like I'm a bug.

Latika takes me aside. She says, "The magazines with Bollywood stars looking like goddesses on the covers sell the fastest, so put those on top."

I rearrange as Latika suggests, and she's right! I sell one magazine to a man who tells me to keep the change.

The change is almost five rupees. Latika says that is mine to keep. I don't need to give that to the newsstand owner.

But then, for the next hour, I don't sell anything more. I leap forward too soon, and a car swerves within inches of my feet. The driver honks, and my trembling hands drop all my magazines.

I watch Latika. The smile on her face is bright even while she is hot and sweaty. She skips to the cars even when she must be scared by how close they are. She tilts her head sweetly when she talks, even if a minute later her shoulders sag in fatigue. She is full of fake happy energy.

I don't know how she can be so cheerful when it's ninety degrees and the humidity threatens to drown us. How does she do this day after day?

Between stoplights, Latika and I sit on the curb. She points to a girl across the street with a baby on her hip, who sells strings of jasmines and little flower posies to offer at temples.

"People buy more flowers from her," says Latika. "They feel bad that she has a baby."

The girl looks like she's only a little older than Latika and Sanjay. Sixteen or seventeen.

By lunch I have sold a few more magazines, and together we've gone through our first batch. We cross the street to the magazine stall to get more. The man gives us a new stack— and also a packet of food made by his wife.

"How nice of him, Latika," I say.

"He's a generous man. He brings me food lots of days," Latika says. "And it's delicious."

I take the first bite of upma and have to agree.

As we eat, Latika says, "I'm surprised you came with me today, Minni, since I know you have other dreams."

I decide to be honest and tell her how difficult everything has become since my mother left. "I was also afraid to go to school today because there was a test," I tell her. "Science is hard to understand when you're not in class, and I've missed a lot. So I didn't want to go and fail the quiz."

"School felt too difficult for me too, so that's why I quit," says Latika. "Everyone thinks I'm stupid because I can't read."

"But you're smart," I tell Latika. "You know how to deal with all kinds of people, and you're good at math."

"I know. It's just that when I try to read, the letters dance on the page. They said I needed special classes, but there was nowhere nearby for me to get them. I had no choice, but you do," Latika says. "Promise me you'll go to school tomorrow. I'll even fill a bucket of water for you."

Latika's words give me a pang. I feel guilty that I thought dropping out of school was easier than staying in. Selling magazines for the day with Latika has opened my eyes to how hard so many people I know work. There are the aunties who make naans, pickles, and sweets over hot stoves. The ones who sew clothes all day, bent over sewing machines in cramped quarters. The men and boys who work in tanning factories with dangerous chemicals. Or work all day and into the night at food stalls, like my baba. Often they get so little in return. All because they don't have an education.

I owe it to my family and friends to not give up.

I promise her that tomorrow I will be in school.

- 30 -

We are almost home when Aisha, a friend of Latika's, joins us.

"Hope you sold a lot of magazines today," she says. "Minni, I didn't know you worked with Latika."

"Just for today," I mumble.

Aisha grabs Latika's hand. "Did you hear about Ravi?"

I stop walking and stare at her. I've been trying hard not to think about the night of the water theft. Aisha saying Ravi's name aloud brings up the darkness and the terror.

But Ravi is a common name—there could be more than one Ravi living in our neighborhood, so maybe I'm jumping to conclusions.

Cautiously I ask, "Which Ravi?"

"The one who works with the government—he lived over in the lane near the market," she says.

My stomach lurches. "I know him. He's a good guy. What happened?" I manage to ask.

"It's terrible. He was found in a gutter near the creek," Aisha says. "My mother knows Ravi's mother well, and of course his parents are heartbroken. They were so proud that he had a government job."

"That's horrible," says Latika. "I know his mother too. My mother and I will visit her."

"That's so sad," I add. I think about how lucky Sanjay and Amit were that Ravi protected them. They have a lot to thank him for, and now they'll never have a chance.

I feel like crying for so many reasons as we cross the busy street toward home.

"My mother said I shouldn't gossip about this, but I can tell you—there are rumors we don't believe—that he died because he drank some homemade alcohol that was toxic," Aisha says.

"Thanks for filling me in," Latika says.

My mind is whirling now. Does this mean that Sanjay can return home? Ravi was the one who helped him and Amit—but he was also the one who recognized them. Now that Ravi is gone, are the boys no longer in danger of being recognized?

That would be the best outcome of this sad news.

- 31 -

It's never a good sign to find Baba home in the middle of the day, so I'm worried when I find him there. It means he either closed the tea stall or asked someone else to mind the stall—two things he hates to do.

Something serious has to be up.

Then I see Amit's uncle here too. He hasn't been by since the day Amit and Sanjay had to leave. Maybe he's heard about Ravi too, and they're planning Sanjay and Amit's return? Part of me feels selfish for not being more upset by Ravi's death. But I can feel a bubble of hope rise within me.

"Baba," I say. "You heard about Ravi?"

"Yes," Ram Uncle answers grimly. "It's why I'm here."

"They say he drank bad liquor and died," I say.

"Who told you that?" Baba and Uncle exchange a look. Baba's tone makes me doubt Aisha's information. "Who?" he asks again.

"A friend of Latika's," I say.

Baba paces around the small room like a caged animal who wants to burst free.

Ram Uncle says, "Did you know that Ravi never drank alcohol? He was a teetotaler."

Baba sits back down. "He had taken a vow at a temple."

I take in their words. "But then how did he die? He was young and healthy. And why are people saying he was drunk, if he didn't drink?"

Baba stops pacing. "Because he's not here to say that he wasn't."

"Everyone says Ravi was a good guy," says Ram Uncle. "But maybe he was tempted to join the wrong crowd. Maybe he was threatened."

I shiver. The people we saw him with that night were certainly the wrong kind of people.

Amit's uncle must read my thoughts. "He wasn't with good people the night our boys saw him. Maybe Ravi made a mistake. He got involved with the wrong people, but then he tried to get out."

"Yes," says Ram Uncle. "Then, when he tried to leave, he paid the biggest price."

So this is how dangerous the water mafia is. Who are these monsters who'll stop at nothing to protect themselves and their crimes?

"I thought maybe that Sanjay and Amit could come home," I mumble.

Now Ram Uncle laughs. "No," he says. "I came to tell your

father that we were right in making the boys leave. That they should definitely not return for a while. Who knows if Ravi said anything to anybody."

I'm taken back to Baba's lesson to not see, hear, or speak evil. We didn't choose to see evil, though. We stumbled upon it. But we were too curious, and it bit us.

"Why can't the police find these people? Punish them?" I ask.

"Because they're so powerful that the authorities look the other way," Ram Uncle says. "They rule people with money, bribes, and paybacks. They are just about impossible to fight."

I think about Sanjay all afternoon as I work at Anita Ma'am's house, even as I dust, sweep and mop floors, and massage Anita Ma'am's feet. I need to talk to him, hear his voice call me Minni Meow. Hear him assure me that he's safe.

Anita Ma'am actually notices. "Meena," she says, "are you okay? Have you talked to your mother? How is she?"

"Yes," I tell her. "She's feeling better. I'm hoping and praying that she'll come home soon."

"We are too, Meena," Anita Ma'am says. "We are too!"

I'm starting to make the dough for rotis when I sense someone standing behind me.

It's Pinky's grandmother. She leans forward, her hands on her hips, and declares, "Not enough oil in that flour."

My hands fumble. I added the amount Ma taught me, so I don't know what to do.

I look over at Anita Ma'am, but she doesn't say anything.

"Add more oil," Grandmother orders.

With shaking hands, I measure a teaspoonful and add it.

"And knead the dough for a full five minutes. Don't be lazy. That's why your rotis are hard."

Pinky's grandmother continues to stand there and tap her foot as I knead. Is she timing me?

After a bit, I look over at Anita Ma'am again.

This time she says, "Mom, Meena is trying. Maybe you should go watch TV."

"All right, but the girl certainly has a lot to learn," she says as she noisily walks out of the kitchen.

I throw a thankful look at Anita Ma'am and finally breathe easy. The rotis *are* softer. Ma always said experienced cooks didn't need the extra oil. But I am nowhere near as skilled as Ma. Will I ever be?

ALL MY THINKING about Sanjay must've somehow reached him. He calls me that night. "Minni Meow!" he yells into my ear, his voice bursting with joy and pride. "Today I cooked for Amit's relatives and some of their friends. I made them my chicken curry—and my famous okra. They loved it!"

"Of course they loved it. I wish I had some right now! Do you remember the last time you brought home leftovers from the restaurant—it was your famous curry, and boy, was it good!" I am thinking back to a night not that long ago and a lifetime ago.

Sanjay starts laughing. "I remember you licking your fingers."

My mouth waters at the memory.

"What did you have for dinner?" he asks.

"Not your chicken curry," I say.

"Minni, make sure you eat. Okay?" he says. "You have a lot to do."

"Aren't you saying I have a lot on my plate? Just not food," I joke, and it feels good to make Sanjay laugh.

Before we hang up, Sanjay tells me how much fun he is having cooking with so many fresh ingredients from the farm. He sounds so happy that I don't want to ruin his mood telling him about Ravi's death. But I decide I had better because I know he'll hear it eventually from Baba or Amit's uncle.

Also, I've learned that our father's advice about trying not to see, hear, or speak about evil, like the three monkeys, isn't always possible or helpful. Bad stuff happens no matter what.

Sanjay listens, and when I'm done, he gives a heavy sigh. "Oh, poor Ravi," he says. "At first I didn't understand why they sent us away; it all seemed so drastic then. But I understand now. I wouldn't have wanted Amit and me to end up like Ravi."

I shudder at the thought. It's hard to believe that this afternoon I was dreaming of Sanjay coming home. Now I'm thankful that he's far away and safe.

- 33 -

The next morning, I wake up before the sun. Rubbing my sleep-swollen eyes, I go out and gather the water. When I return home, Latika is there to help. She says she will finish boiling the water. "Go," she says. "Go to school, Minni. For me and for you."

I kiss her as I fly out the door.

I race to meet Faiza at our usual place—and she's there! When she sees me, she hugs me tight. "Minni, you came."

When Shiva sees us, he says, "Minni, I'm happy you're back."

"Me too," I say. "I'm going to try even harder not to miss any more school."

We pass some girls who seem surprised to see me. "Minni, we thought you were working as a servant now."

"Oh, that's not full-time—it's just for some extra cash," I say casually, and I'm proud of myself. The old Minni would've been upset to have everyone all up in my business. But this is small stuff. I know there are a lot of bigger worries.

Miss Shah greets me with a small wave, and I wave back. When she takes roll call and I shout, "Present!" she flashes the brightest smile.

It feels good to hear the chalk squeak as Miss Shah writes math problems on the blackboard. It feels good to hear pages rustle and see Faiza bent over her notebook across the aisle.

It feels good to sharpen my pencil and solve the worksheet that Miss Shah has assigned. My brain is snapping to attention. Like it's back on duty.

It even feels good to sneeze when Miss Shah makes a dust cloud while cleaning the chalkboard eraser.

At the end of the day, Miss Shah calls me to her desk. "I'm happy that you came back, Minni. I was afraid you wouldn't. That you might have to drop out like so many others. Is there anything I can do to help you till your mother returns?"

I can't think of anything, so I shake my head.

"Well, if you need help with any of the science concepts, I'm happy to explain after class," she says as she puts a hand on my shoulder. "You know, I had to work as a kid too while I was going to school. And I grew up in a pretty similar neighborhood."

Really? I would never have guessed at all.

"We working girls have to help each other," Miss Shah says. Her kindness and her concern bring a lump to my throat.

"Minni, have you thought of boiling the water at night?" she says. "Faiza says it's slowing you down in the morning."

"That's a good idea," I tell her. "I thought I'd be too tired after school and my job, but at least I have more time then."

Why hadn't I thought of this? With Ma gone, nobody really needs water during the day. I wonder what else I am not figuring out because I'm always exhausted or in a hurry.

"I know there's a lot to figure out, Minni," Miss Shah says. "Just take it one day at a time. Each day is a small victory. Celebrate that."

THAT NIGHT, I think about how Miss Shah was once a poor kid like me. Seeing how far she has come gives me hope. But at the same time, I wish Latika and people like us were given more support to be *able* to stay in school. A poem starts to form, and I write in my notebook:

They say numbers don't lie.
Ma dropped out of school in 5th grade,
Baba left school in the 6th,
Naan Aunty had to stay home after 4th.
Latika stayed home after 6th.
Numbers, they say, don't lie.
But do they always add up?

Did all these people really drop out?

Or were they pushed?

Did Life give them any choice?

Numbers, they say, don't lie.

But do they tell the story?

- 34 -

The minute I enter Pinky's house, I know something is different. The dining table is set, and a feast is being prepared in the kitchen. Anita Ma'am is all dressed up and stirring a pot of goat curry. "It's my husband's favorite."

"He's here?" I ask.

"Yes," she replies. "He's home for a late lunch."

I've never seen Pinky's father except in that photo in Anita Ma'am's room.

"Meena," Anita Ma'am says, "today the rotis should be perfect like your mother's. Make the dough now and then you can cook them right before we sit down—my husband likes them hot off the pan."

I nod and prepare the dough with the extra oil to make it softer, while Lata and Anita Ma'am scurry around the kitchen making sure the goat curry, the vegetables, the raita, the rice, and the fried poppadums are perfect. Anita Ma'am tastes all the dishes to adjust the spice and salt levels for her husband like he's royalty.

When he arrives, I am told it is time to heat the pan for the rotis. While I've improved a lot in the past weeks, I'm nowhere near as fast as my mother. I remember her telling us about how her hands could roll a perfect roti every minute for Pinky's father. She said he would thank her with tips, which she promptly added to her savings jar.

I try, but I can't roll out thin rotis this fast. They come out thick and uneven, but Lata dabs them with ghee and runs them into the adjacent dining room.

We hear Anita Ma'am's voice. "Bring another batch of roti," she says.

I'm sweating heavily as I cook a few more. They are not much better—not a perfect circle among them.

Lata looks concerned when she returns. "Meena," she whispers, "are you okay?"

I hear the grandmother say, "This roti cannot be for my son. It's horrible. Let's eat some rice instead."

I turn off the stove with relief.

A few minutes later, Anita Ma'am calls out, "Meena, you can bring us the pudding now."

Lata has placed the pudding on a pretty tray with a lace cloth underneath it. I lift it carefully and walk out into the dining room.

Pinky is looking at me and smiling. She must be happy her father is home.

But her father is not happy. "Did she make those rotis?" he barks at Anita Ma'am. "What kind of servants are you hiring these days?"

"That's exactly what I've been saying," his mother pipes in.

I turn to look at the father's face and notice the white scar on his cheek. It's the same mark I saw on the face of the man who chased Sanjay and Amit by the train tracks.

I stare at the scar as if hypnotized.

Then he stares back at me. "What are you looking at? Do I know you?"

I manage to shake my head. "No, sahib."

His face is red, and the vein at his temple beats. "Girl, are you going to serve that or stand there?"

His voice creeps up my spine and chokes me. I've heard that voice before, in my nightmares. The voice is always harsh and croaky, and it's drowned out by the sounds of an oncoming train hurtling down the tracks. Just before it runs over Sanjay, I wake up.

But this is not a nightmare. It's real life. And Pinky's father is . . . *that* man! A criminal who steals water in the dead of the night.

He's also the person who may be responsible for Ravi's death.

The bowl of pudding falls out of my hands and onto the floor. The milky dessert splatters all over the room. The glass bowl is splintered into a million pieces that can jab and cut.

Anita Ma'am, her mother-in-law, and her husband all

jump up. Everyone is shouting and screaming as if I've spilled hot coals.

Pinky's father storms off, and her grandmother steps on a glass splinter.

"Lata, Lata," Anita Ma'am calls, "come help me."

When I move to try to clean up, Anita Ma'am shoos me away.

"Just leave," she says. "Leave. You've done enough."

I catch a glimpse of Pinky. Her eyes are wide, and her hands cover her mouth in shock. She has seen my humiliation.

I turn and run as fast as I can out of their building and only stop when I'm close to home.

This day was *not* any kind of victory. Today I came face-to-face with the monster.

- 35 -

Instead of going home, I run straight to Faiza's house. She is the only other person I can talk to who was with me that night and who is still in Mumbai.

As I near her house, I call out to her, "Faiza! Faiza!"

Her mother steps out. "Minni?" she says, a look of concern on her face. "What happened?"

"Nothing," I lie. "Nothing."

I realize I must act normal even if my life has burst open like a storm cloud.

Faiza's ammi gives me a look and calls Faiza. When Faiza sees the panicked look in my eyes, she calmly gets her backpack and tells her mother, "We're going to study at Minni's."

Once we're out of earshot, she says, "What happened?"

I'm shaking. "I met that boss man from that night."

She stops walking. "What? Where?"

I grab her hand. "Faiza, you'll never believe this, but he lives in Pinky's house."

Faiza looks at me like I've gone mad.

"That man is her father," I say.

I wait for her to take that in. Faiza keeps staring at me, and I nod. "He's her father. Anita Ma'am's husband," I repeat as if to convince myself and her.

"Are you sure?" she says. "How could it be?"

"I'm sure," I say. "He's not a businessman. He is a water thief. A common robber."

"Who lives in a fancy building," finishes Faiza. "Did he have that scar on his cheek?"

I nod. "And that rough voice too, like he has a cough."

"But he didn't recognize you, right?"

"I don't think so," I say. "He was looking at Sanjay and Amit, and we were in the shadows."

Faiza exhales. She hugs me. "Minni, I don't know what I'd do if you were in danger too."

"I don't think I am. But when I stared at him, he did ask if he knew me. Of course I told him no . . ."

"Pray that he never remembers," she says.

"I think I've lost Ma's job. I made such a huge mess! My mother is going to be so upset. She counted on Anita Ma'am and this job."

"Did they tell you not to come?" she asks.

"No, but Pinky's father stormed off, and I think the grand-mother stepped on the broken glass. Then Anita Ma'am asked me to leave. She didn't want me causing more damage."

Faiza tries to hide a smile. "Oh, Minni, this would be

funny if parts of it weren't so serious. And it serves that evil grandmother right. I think you should just go tomorrow and hope for the best. Pinky's father won't be there, right?"

"No. But what am I supposed to do now that I know he's a criminal?" I ask.

"We have to be careful. Very careful. Remember what happened to Ravi. Let's think on it, but for now don't tell anyone."

Then Faiza takes off the black cord with the amulet on it that her grandmother gave her to protect her from evil. "Wear this for now," she says as she puts it around my neck.

"Thank you, Faiza. You really are the best friend ever," I tell her.

We should be studying, but we're too revved up, so we walk over to Shanti's.

Shanti greets us with a smile. "I didn't think I would see you girls with exams so close."

"We're taking a break," says Faiza.

"And something we read made us wonder," I say. "Do you think it's possible for a regular person to defeat a big, powerful person?"

"Why not?" Shanti says. "Remember the story of the foolish lion?"

"I do," says Faiza. "He ordered the animals to offer themselves as prey, one a day, or he would destroy the jungle."

"The animals obeyed," I say. "Till it was rabbit's turn." The story comes back to me. The rabbit arrives late, saying he barely escaped from a much bigger lion, making the lion furious. When the old lion asks to meet the bigger lion, the rabbit takes him to a deep well. Upon seeing his reflection, the foolish lion pounces at it, falls in the well, and drowns.

"Is there a lion you need to tell me about, girls?" Shanti asks.

Faiza replies instantly, "No, Shanti."

But Shanti's smart and knows we're hiding something. She says, "You know if you are in trouble I'm always here to help, right?"

We don't want to get Shanti in trouble. Telling her the details about that night and Pinky's father's identity would get her involved.

I need to be as smart as the rabbit who outwitted the king of the jungle. It seems possible in a story, but this is the real world. Pinky's father is not as dumb as the old lion; in fact, he is cunning.

But the story reminds me that in an unequal battle, the less powerful person can use their wits to find a way. It has happened before and can happen again!

- 36 -

Not even the computer class can make me stop thinking about Pinky's father.

Sanjay called last night, and he too agreed that we had to stay calm and take time to think of a way out. "Minni," he promised, "I'll call again soon. Don't do anything foolish. He can crush you like an ant beneath his foot."

"Thanks, Sanjay!" I said. I already felt like an ant; I didn't need the image of someone crushing me.

"Minni!" Priya Didi calls out. "Where are you today?"

"Sorry," I say, and I try to make myself focus.

Today she's explaining that apps are computer programs that make life easier and help us solve problems.

"What are some common problems that you face?" she asks the class. "And then let's see if we can dream up an app to fix it."

Priya Didi starts to make a list on the board, but I'm pretty sure my problems are hopeless. I don't think there's an app that can salvage Ma's job, bring my brother back, and catch a criminal.

Gita raises her hand. "Priya Didi," she says, "my parents can speak some English but can't read or write it too well. I taught them to write their names in English. Can I make an app to teach them? They want to learn, but they are embarrassed to go to classes."

I understand this issue. Neither of my parents can read very well. Ma reads some Hindi, but Baba always hands Ma things that need to be read.

Like me, so many of the other girls know how this feels.

Shanti agrees. "Good one," she says as she takes out her conch shell and blows it, which makes us all giggle.

Amina raises her hand and starts off by saying, "It may be a silly idea, but—"

Before she can continue, Priya Didi interrupts her. "Remember, all ideas are good. Now go ahead."

"Okay. So when I'm walking around alone, I'm scared," she says. "What if someone attacks me?"

Priya Didi says, "I think we all feel that way sometimes. What would the app do?"

"Could we build an app to keep us safe when we are walking alone?" Amina asks. "Maybe a loud alarm could go off when you press a button?"

"And maybe when you hit the alarm, it can call an emergency contact," Gita says.

Priya Didi gives them both a high five, and we're all excited now.

Technology can give us power. I feel like the goddess Shakti, who fights evil and sometimes rides a tiger, instead of powerless me.

The discussion goes on. Ideas pour out. Someone says that we should make an app to send our pictures of local garbage heaps to the Municipal Corporation so that we badger them enough that they finally do something about it.

Others talk of figuring out ways to bring volunteers together to clean up our rivers and beaches.

The clouds are lifting like they do on days after a downpour of rain. The sun peeks out, and the sky becomes yellow and orange.

I'm starting to feel like the smart rabbit in the story. Maybe there is a way out.

"What if there was a way for people to report things to the police," I say aloud, "but without anyone knowing who you are?"

Shanti's head shoots up. She looks at me with suspicion.

"You mean anonymously?" asks Priya Didi.

"Yes," I say. Now I'm not sure if I should've asked the question.

"An app would help solve that problem," says Priya Didi.

When the class is done, Shanti comes to me, and she links her hand in mine to walk home together.

The late-April heat rises through the pavement. There's been no rain, and the headlines in the newspaper continue to talk about the low levels in the lakes. But I don't need to read the newspaper to know the water supply has been cut. The lines at the taps tell me.

"Minni," Shanti says, "I know it's difficult not having your mother here now. I just want to make sure that you know that you can come to me for anything."

I know I can, but I couldn't live with myself if something happened to her because of me. Shanti is needed by the whole community. Not only for all she does at the community center, but she's also the best shoulder to cry on, and her stories keep us going.

"I know that," I finally say. "And I'm grateful."

"Then don't say anything," she says. "Just nod."

I nod.

"Do you know something that no one else knows?" she asks.

I nod.

"Could it get you in trouble?" she asks.

I nod vigorously.

"Please, Minni, if you ever feel like you are in danger, please promise you'll come to me? You can answer me now."

"Yes," I tell her. "I promise if that happens, I will."

"Good," Shanti says. "We both know that you're brave, Minni, but lately I've seen just how thoughtful and smart you are too. You can do anything you want—maybe with computers, or maybe you'll discover something you love even better. Your future is bright; don't forget that in all your worries."

Shanti's words echo what Sanjay has told me.

If they believe in me, then shouldn't I believe in myself too?

- 37 -

I'M feeling nervous as I ring the doorbell at Anita Ma'am's house. Will she send me home? Will I be officially fired? At least I will know one way or the other because I dared to show up.

But she doesn't look angry and asks me to come in.

Pinky's grandmother sits on the couch in the living room. The stern expression on her face makes me want to sink through the floor. "Anita," she prompts her daughter-in-law. "Remember what we discussed."

"Meena," Anita Ma'am says, "I must say that I expected more from you. I believed Rohini when she said you were trained and a good worker, when that was clearly not the case."

I stare at my toes. I know better than to say anything to defend Ma or myself. I hear her telling me to not speak unless necessary.

Pinky's grandmother says, "If you worked for me, I'd make

you pay for the bowl you broke, even if it took you a year to pay. Anita needs to be more careful when she hires servants."

She tsks and gets up. The doorway to the living room is narrow, and she gestures for me to move out of her way. I shrink into the wall. Is she afraid to get too close to me or touch me because I'm from a lower caste? Some people say those old beliefs died years ago, but I am learning that's not the case.

"One more mistake, and I'll have to let you go," Anita Ma'am says. "I'm letting you stay because Rohini is such a good worker and I hope that she'll be back soon."

I'm hoping Ma is back soon too.

I am so close to tears that I rush into the kitchen to gather myself before I start cleaning. I am glad to hear that Pinky is staying late at school today so I can focus on my work.

The TV blares in the background as I clean the living room. Anita Ma'am is sitting on the couch and supervising me as she does, while also reading a film magazine.

I'm mopping the floor when I hear the news commentator say that police are on the heels of gangs that are stealing water from tanker trucks and private wells.

I stop and wring the mop. I sneak a glance at Anita Ma'am. She's lying on the couch, deep into her magazine.

Suddenly she raises herself on an elbow and says, "Did you know that they're going to be filming a big-budget movie on Juhu Beach next month?" Then she sinks back down on the couch.

No, I did not, and I don't care. Do you know that your husband is a water thief?

I wring the cloth mop again and again, as if I could wring the truth from it.

"Meena," she says, "did you clean that corner? Yesterday my mother-in-law noticed some dust."

I go back to the corner and mop the floor as hard as possible. The scrubbing is helping me not scream.

Now the news commentator is saying that police are asking citizens to help with identifying the water thieves. Phone numbers to report crimes flash on the screen. They are big and bold, and I try to memorize them but know I should write them down. The number keeps flashing, and I reach for the paper and pencil that sits on the side table. In my rush, I stumble, the edge of the table hits my elbow, and I gasp in pain.

Anita Ma'am gives me a puzzled look but is more interested in her magazine, and now I'm thankful for movie stars and their fascinating lives.

I manage to scribble down two of the three phone numbers on the screen.

I LEAVE WORK and head to Faiza's house. We tell her mom we're going for a walk, and when we are outside, I thrust the paper with the numbers into Faiza's hand and explain.

"We don't have a phone, so how can we call?" Faiza asks.

"Let's think," I say. "We can't really borrow a phone from our parents, because who knows how long it will take to reach the tip line."

"A private place would be good," Faiza adds.

We're walking past the community center when I see Priya Didi in the window.

I grab Faiza's hand, and we walk into the center.

"Priya Didi," I say. "We need to make a call, but we don't have a phone."

She raises an eyebrow. Then she stands up and tugs her phone out of her jeans pocket. She offers it to me without any questions.

"It might take a little time," Faiza says. I nod.

"I'm here for a while," she says. "Go to the back room."

Faiza and I both hug Priya Didi tight. "Go," she says. "Go."

In the back room, between piles of boxes and chairs, I dial the number.

When the phone rings and I hear a voice, I get goose bumps. But then I realize that it's not a human. It's a recording that tells us that the phone will be answered when it's our turn, and then music plays.

Faiza and I hold our ears to the phone, waiting. We jump when we finally hear a live voice say, "Mumbai Police."

"Sir," I say. "I have a tip about the water thieves."

Before I can say any more, he asks, "How old are you?"

Without thinking, I answer, "Twelve, sir."

"Hey, listen, everyone, now a twelve-year-old is calling. She knows something the police doesn't," he says, and starts cracking up. I hear others laughing in the background too.

Then he hangs up. The call is over. There's silence.

Faiza and I look at each other in disbelief.

Listen to me, I want to scream into the disconnected phone. *I may be only twelve, but I've seen a world of trouble. Isn't it time you grown-ups* do *something about it?*

- 38 -

In Pinky's room I change her sheets while she sits at her desk, studying. As I smooth the sheets, I notice a picture tacked onto her bulletin board. I know it wasn't there before. It's a photo of Pinky with her parents in front of snow-topped mountains. Next to it is a smaller photo of just her father standing with his hands on his hips.

She notices me looking and says, "We took that picture when we went to Switzerland last year."

Then Pinky points to a cardboard box overflowing with photos on her floor. "Will you put those away?" she says. "I found the ones I needed."

I nod, and my mind starts racing. Maybe that box has more pictures of her father. What if I took one and got it to the police to help identify him? Except how would I get it to them?

When I finish making Pinky's bed, I kneel on the floor, facing away from Pinky, and start gathering up the photos. Most of them are of Anita Ma'am and Pinky. But then I see a copy of the picture of Pinky's father that's on the bulletin board, and I quickly slide it into my shirt.

She has so many photos, she'll never miss a copy.

LATER, AS I head home, I wonder, *Am I a thief?* But all I stole is a copy of a photo, not something precious like water, which we all need to live.

My theft is not hurting people.

Instead I'm trying to help. Somehow I need to get the photo to someone important, like a journalist. Maybe Faiza and I can find the address for a newspaper office or TV station. Then we could take the bus there and give the photo to someone. But would they laugh their heads off when they see we're twelve-year-olds, just like the police did?

My stomach rumbles, and I realize that I'm hungry, so I decide to swing by Baba's tea stall. As I near it, I see two men in police uniforms, and for an absurd moment, I think they're there to arrest me for my theft.

But the men look happy as Baba chats away with them. They don't seem like the policeman on the phone.

Baba sees me and smiles. "This is my daughter, Minni," he tells the officers.

"Your father makes the best chai," one of them says. "It's strong and sweet."

"I need a cup every day around this time so I don't fall asleep on duty," the other says.

"You also seem to need plenty of pakodas. Do they help you stay awake too?" the first one teases him.

When the policemen leave, I ask Baba, "Do they come every day?"

"Yes, they do," he says. "They're my regulars at this hour."

"That's nice," I say. And it is, especially because now it seems I have a possible solution right in front of me.

- 39 -

The next day, doubts fill my head. Why do I think I can change anything? Who am I? A mere twelve-year-old girl who is struggling to pass seventh grade. Whose family is just scraping by in this city of millions.

Then I remember all the fights I've witnessed in the water lines.

When there's not enough water to go around, there's anger, fear, and frustration. All it takes is a mere spark for fights to flare up. Just the other day I heard that a child was hurt when someone accused her mother of cutting the line. The little girl was caught in the wrong place at the wrong time, like Naan Aunty's husband. Trouble found her through no fault of her own.

I think of Pinky's father. People like him make a bad situation worse, all so that they can get rich. They care nothing about us.

I can't back away. I have to act, to do something.

I FIND FAIZA after work. She uses her left hand to write Pinky's father's name and address on the back of the picture, and I use mine to write *Water Thief.* The plan is to slip it into one of the policemen's bags when they are too busy talking to notice us.

We wait till the sun is setting, which is when the policemen come for their cup of chai.

I feel stronger wearing Sanjay's T-shirt and with Faiza by my side. The T-shirt smells faintly of him and of the lemon-scented soap Ma—and now I—use to wash our clothes. The picture is in the pocket of my skirt in an envelope. Moti is by our side too.

I gnaw at the nail on my index finger. My new habit of biting my nails whenever I'm anxious or scared is a painful one, and I'm surprised I have any nails left.

I stare at my hands. They look different. All the mopping and scrubbing have hardened my skin and given me calluses. Then I notice my hands now look like Ma's and Baba's and Sanjay's. Working hands. That makes me proud of them.

We walk by a group of Amit's friends rapping a popular song. "Our time will come," they sing. "Our time will come."

Faiza pokes me and says, "Hopefully, Boss Man's time has come too," and her joke eases the tension.

WHEN WE ARRIVE at Baba's stall, I see a bunch of policemen in their khaki uniforms. They are chatting about their new police chief as they sip their chai, saying how he's been brought in to shake things up, that he's tough but fair.

Part of me wants to race back home. What would Baba think about what I'm planning to do? He doesn't even know that Pinky's father is a criminal. But if he did, would he understand that I'm acting in a smart and cautious way? That I'm not looking for trouble, but instead trying to help get rid of it?

Sensing my fears, Faiza whispers, "You can do this, Minni. Remember, you're the smart rabbit."

"Thanks, Faiza," I say. "It is now or never, so I better get moving."

She smiles at my lousy joke, and we start to walk over to Baba, but we turn around when we see Moti isn't following us.

Instead, he goes up to the policeman and wags his tail. One of them reaches down and strokes him. "Who is this?" he asks.

Faiza walks over and says, "He's Moti. The best dog in the world."

Everyone is focused on Moti. No one is looking at me.

It's a perfect moment. Faiza is now asking the policemen about their work.

I get close to one of them and drop the picture into the bag hanging on his shoulder.

It slips in.

Just like that.

It's done.

"Minni," Baba says, and gives me two cups of tea. My hands tremble as I accept them, but luckily Baba is too busy to notice. As I pass one over to Faiza, our eyes meet, and Faiza winks.

We're both giddy as we walk home.

"Moti," I say, "has anyone ever told you that you are the best dog in the whole world?"

"I just did a minute ago!" Faiza laughs. "I'm going to be telling him that all the time!"

When we get home, we find a biscuit for Moti—Moti, the wonder dog and our secret weapon.

I am walking by the community center when I hear a voice say, "Are you Rohini's daughter?" It's the new doctor that Ma saw at the clinic before she left for the village.

"Yes," I say.

"I've been waiting for your mother to come back to see me. I have the results of her blood tests." Seeing my blank look, she says, "Weren't you with her the day I did a blood test on your mother?"

"Oh yes," I tell her. "I just forgot because that seems so long ago now. Right after seeing you, my ma left to go to her mother's house, where she could get more rest. She's starting to feel better."

"That's good news," she says. "Can you come inside the clinic now for a minute so we can talk privately?"

The doctor sounds so serious that all my fears wake up. What did the blood tests show?

"Does she have cancer?" I ask as soon as we get inside. "Is she going to die?"

The doctor motions for me to sit down across from her and quickly begins to explain. "No, she doesn't have cancer. And if she did, there are things we can do for that now. But your mother does have hepatitis A. It's treatable."

I hear the word *treatable*, and I start inhaling again.

"Hepatitis is a liver infection caused by a virus. It spreads from contaminated food or water. Do you boil your water?"

Water, water, water. It's always about the water.

"Yes, we always do now," I tell her. "But there were times when we were too busy . . ."

"Well, I am glad you're always boiling it now," the doctor says. "So the good news for your mother is that in most cases, the patient heals with time and rest. But there is a vaccine that the rest of your family should get as soon as possible."

"If we get the vaccine, we won't get it?" I ask.

"That's right," she says. "Just like polio and smallpox, hepatitis A has a vaccine."

I nod. Tears of relief flow down my face freely. That sounds so simple. Why didn't we know this?

I thank the doctor and sprint to Baba's stall to tell him the good news. I pump my arms and wish they were wings. I feel the burn in my calves. I can't get there fast enough.

When I tell him everything the doctor said, Baba's face lifts in a smile. All of a sudden he looks years younger. We were all equally worried. Baba, Sanjay, and I were all so scared for Ma and afraid to talk about our fear.

"Let's call your ma right now," he says, and hands me the phone. "You tell her."

And after I do, I can hear the relief in Ma's voice too. "I'm really going to be fine," she says happily.

Then I rush to tell Faiza and her mother and the rest of our neighbors.

Faiza's mother hugs me. Shanti's smile trembles when I tell her. And Naan Aunty says, "Praise God, Minni."

They all had been worried too.

When a fear is too terrifying, I realize, we are scared to give it words, as if that will make it all too real. But the anxiety doesn't go away. It's like a weed that continues to grow, sprout, and choke the plant.

Late that night, I talk to Sanjay and fill him in on Ma's health report.

"Minni," he says, "you've given me the best news ever."

It always feels so good to make my brother happy.

Then I tell him about the photograph and how Moti helped Faiza and me secretly deliver it to the policeman. "You three are brilliant," my brother says, and when I ask him to repeat that, he laughs loud and hard.

That night, I write in my journal.

Shanti tells me water has many names
in many languages.

water, paani, eau,
H_2O, rain, jal,
maa, agua, nero,
neer, vatten, voda,
and others that I don't know.
But I do know water is life.
It flows, falls, rolls, collects, storms, and drips.
Like life, it is always changing.
But at this moment it feels like my glass is full
and I am thankful.

- 41 -

A couple days later as I return from work, I see Naan Aunty. "Namaste, Minni," she says, and gives me a knowing smile.

Moti comes running toward me as I near our house, his tail wagging in circles. "You look happy too," I say.

As I get closer, I breathe in the familiar aroma of daal.

Ma is home! I know it even before I enter the house.

Ma sees me and drops the sari she's folding, reaches for me, and gives me the longest hug. I breathe in the familiar rose scent of her soap.

Wrapped in her arms, I let go of all the worry I've been holding in—about not enough water, school, Ma's health, and my job.

Baba comes home for dinner. Ma turns on the radio, and she hums along as old Bollywood songs play in the background. Baba joins in too, but he is so off-key that we start laughing.

"The village might've been quieter, but I missed you. I'll take the noise of home," she says.

We sit on the floor in our little circle, and I savor *everything*.

It's a simple meal, daal and rice. Nothing like the elaborate meals with meats and several vegetables I serve at Pinky's house. But I wouldn't trade it for anything.

That night, I message Sanjay on Baba's phone:

Ma is home.

That sentence alone is poetry.

THE NEXT DAY, Ma insists that I accompany her to Anita Ma'am's house and say goodbye even though that's the last thing I want to do. Going to work the last few days has been scary. I've been so afraid that my guilt would be visible like a badge on my shirt. I also worried that Pinky's father might show up again. I don't know what I'd do if I had to face him again. It didn't end well last time.

The flame tree near Pinky's apartment has blossomed and is full of gorgeous red flowers, as if it's welcoming Ma back.

Ma grabs my hand and says, "Minni, I'm proud of you for going to work and keeping my job."

I remind myself to say the minimum and just murmur some thanks. I don't want to reveal anything to Ma by accident.

But Ma seems pleased with my response. "Minni, you've really grown up. I worried about you being able to keep quiet. You always had so much to say."

If only she knew the stories that could come flooding out! I'm debating if I should say anything about the spilled pudding and smashed bowl in case Anita Ma'am mentions it, but as we turn the corner, we see three police cars parked in front of Pinky's building. We also see a van belonging to a TV crew setting up cameras.

"What is going on here?" Ma says. "I hope everyone is all right!"

The guard at the gate stops us and says nobody can enter the building till the police give the okay.

We watch as a man dressed in long khaki pants and a matching shirt gets out of one of the police cars and enters the gate. We recognize him. We've seen him on TV. He's the new police chief that the policemen in my father's shop were talking about. The one who is shaking things up and has a reputation for being able to stand up to the corrupt gangs.

Ma keeps craning her neck to look over the gate, and other bystanders join us. Some young boys climb a tree to get a better view. I would like to join them, but Ma grabs my hand and keeps me by her side.

Police gather around the gate. It begins to open, and the TV cameraman rushes closer.

The police chief walks out, and behind him is Pinky's father. In handcuffs. His eyes are focused on the ground. Two other policemen are holding his arms.

The bystanders gasp, and Ma almost faints.

I'm rooted to the street in disbelief. How did this happen?

Did the police already know about Pinky's father from other tips? Maybe the picture I gave them helped too?

I'll never know.

What I do know is that I worked to right a wrong. And that the man who could have crushed us like ants no longer has that power.

- 42 -

The news of Pinky's father being arrested floods the neighborhood like water after a big monsoon rain.

There's disbelief that someone like him could be part of the water mafia. There's shock that someone so rich and powerful could be caught. Many people are jubilant that the police are working for the people and catching real criminals. Others shake their heads and predict lawyers will just get him freed.

I watch the news and read the newspaper. They say they hope that the arrest of Pinky's father will lead to arrests of even bigger bosses. Those who pull the strings from afar.

I'm amazed that there are people more powerful and richer than Pinky's father.

As for Pinky's mother, Ma went to visit her this morning to see how she was doing and to tell her about the hepatitis A, like the doctor advised. But it turns out Anita Ma'am and her whole family have been vaccinated. I guess all the rich people are. At least the doctor said they were working on arranging a free vaccination day in our neighborhood.

Now Ma tells me that when she got there, Anita Ma'am's eyes were swollen from crying and Pinky was trying to comfort her and make her tea. The mother-in-law was gone.

"She is going to go and live with her daughter," Ma says. "Heaven help the daughter."

I start giggling, and Ma joins me. But then I see worry lines crease Ma's forehead. "They'll all be gone soon," she says. "Anita Ma'am is going to move to her mother's house in Pune for a while with Pinky. They have no plans to come back."

So despite all my efforts, Ma lost her job anyway.

"Ma," I say, "what will we do? Anita Ma'am paid my school fees."

"We'll figure something out," Ma says. "Let's not worry too much. I like to believe that when one door closes, another opens."

Does it, though, Ma? I wonder.

I've grown up so much in these weeks that I don't even have to bite my tongue to keep the words I'll regret from blurting out. They simply dance around in my mind.

I decide I *won't* let myself worry too much. If I have to, I'll attend the free government-run school, even though they say that sometimes the teachers don't even show up till the middle of the day. I just need to graduate high school, and I will.

BABA HAS LEFT his phone with us so Sanjay can call, and when the phone rings, I jump on it. "Oh, Sanjay, can you believe they arrested Pinky's father? Maybe there is justice in the world after all. And now you can come home. You and Ma back here will be like a dream come true to me!"

Sanjay is quiet, and in a flash I remember my conversation with Faiza when I just talked and didn't listen. I won't make that mistake again.

"Sorry I'm rambling on, Sanjay. Tell me how you are."

"I'm fine, Minni," he says. "But I've made a big decision."

"You bought a ticket home?"

"No, Minni," he says. "The thing is, I'm not coming home."

"You mean you want to stay there a little longer, Sanjay?" I ask. "I know how much you like it in the country."

"Minni," he says. And something about his tone gives me goose bumps.

"Minni Meow," he starts again. "Remember when I cooked for Amit's family and friends and they loved my food? It turns out one of their friends owns a small restaurant. His cook is leaving, and he offered me the job. I will earn money—and I'll be able to send some of it to help pay for your school fees."

I take that in.

"Thanks, Sanjay, but you don't have to—I'd rather have you home. Maybe your old restaurant here would let you cook one day?"

"One day is not *today*," Sanjay says. "Here I'll be a real cook. In Mumbai, I cut vegetables."

"Right." My voice shakes as I admit this. "You're right."

"This is what I want to do, Minni. You know, you and me, we're both thirsty for more. You for an education, me for an opportunity."

Sanjay is right. We are both thirsty. And it's our time to do the things we want. It's hard realizing that as much as I want Sanjay home, it isn't the best thing for him.

"What about Amit?" I ask, to keep myself from crying.

"He'll be home tomorrow. He can't wait to get back to Mumbai. It's all he talks—and sings—about."

"I'm happy for him," I say. "And you—is there anything at all that you miss about Mumbai?"

"I miss the sound of the ocean. And a pesky little sister who's sometimes a poet. Minni, you know, your poems are really good. I might even have to come up with a new nickname for you now that you're practically all grown up."

"That's a good idea. Remember, you did say I was brilliant—although you said that about Moti too," I joke. "And believe it or not, I might actually miss being called Minni Meow."

Before we say goodbye, he says, "Minni, don't be sad. Be happy for me."

"I am, Sanjay. I really am."

That evening, as Faiza and I study inside, I hear Ma out on the stoop telling Naan Aunty that she needs a job.

"I've tasted your rotis," Naan Aunty tells her. "They're the best. Have you thought of starting a roti business like my naan business?"

"No, I haven't," Ma says. "I'm uneducated. What do I know about a business?"

"Don't say that," Naan Aunty says. "You're smart, and if I could do it, so could you. We may not know how to speak in English, but nobody makes bread as good as ours."

I can hear the excitement in Ma's voice when she asks, "What do I need to do to start it up?"

"Orders from clients," says Naan Aunty. "And of course your hands, some wheat flour, a pinch of salt, and some oil."

I jump up and run outside and say, "You can do it, Ma!"

Naan Aunty flexes her biceps like a bodybuilder, and Ma flexes hers too. It's good to see my mother looking so excited.

"Ma," I say, "I'll help you. I can make flyers to advertise your business. I bet the girls in my computer class will help. And we can ask the nice security man at Pinky's building to give out flyers to all the residents. Faiza and I can distribute them everywhere else."

Ma giggles. "Oh, Minni, I missed your enthusiasm. It would be nice to be my own boss and not have to massage the feet of women who are exhausted from spending their money."

After Naan Aunty leaves, Ma starts to make noodles for me and Faiza. While she's cooking, I walk up behind her and hug her tight. "Thank you, Ma! Thank you for making me noodles!"

Ma looks at me and says, "Maybe I should go away more often. It's just some noodles from a packet."

I want to tell her that I'll never again take for granted her making food for me. Maybe one day I'll even tell her the stories about working at Anita Ma'am's.

While Faiza and I slurp our noodles, I think of Ma's conversation with Naan Aunty. "Hey, Ma," I say. "I think you were right about new doors opening. What do you think about calling your new business Rohini's Rotis?"

"Rohini's Rotis." Ma rolls it around her tongue. "I like that. It has a nice ring to it. And it sure beats being Anita Ma'am's servant!"

- 44 -

On Sunday morning, I'm at the water line to give Ma a day off from fetching it all the time.

The line is long, and some women ahead of me squat on the street instead of standing. Faiza stands in line with me, and we quiz each other. With only a handful of days left before our exam, we're using every minute we have to study.

"What if there was a way to save all this time that we spend in line?" Faiza says as she turns a page in the review packet. "Why don't you come up with your favorite thing—some kind of app—to solve this problem."

"If only I could," I say, but then Faiza's words sink in. "You know what, Faiza, you're brilliant! That's the perfect problem for me to try to solve for computer class. We try to save money, we save food, we save trees. And of course it makes sense to save time too."

"Always glad to be of service," Faiza says, bowing down in front of me before breaking into a dance move.

Later, I burst into computer class. "Priya Didi, I have an idea for an app."

"Tell me," Priya Didi says.

The words tumble out of me. "People can line up for water on my app. When it's their turn, the app will ping on their phones. Then they can pick up their buckets and containers and run to the tap. It will save everyone time. People won't get so irritated. Maybe there will be fewer fights."

Priya Didi claps her hands. "Nice idea—what will you call it?"

It bursts out of my mouth: "Paani."

"Water," says Shanti. "Yes. Water, which is essential to life."

"But, Minni," Gita says, "not everyone has a phone."

"Ah, good point," I admit. "Of course they don't."

"And how will you deal with the people who just line up and don't use the app?" Amina asks.

More good points. I realize I was so excited by the idea that I didn't think it through well enough.

Seeing my disappointed face, Priya Didi says, "Minni, all good ideas come with problems. That's part of the challenge. Your idea is solid. But you have to keep working on all the angles. These are glitches that all our apps will face."

Priya Didi's advice makes me feel better. And after class she stops me to ask how my studying is going.

"Okay, I guess," I tell her, "except that I'm terrible at remembering dates."

"I was too," she says. "But I think I have a solution for *that* problem. What helped me was writing all the important dates in big numbers on index cards, because I'm a visual learner. Want to make some together now?"

"Really, you have time?"

"Sure, plus helping you learn Indian history will help me learn too," says Priya Didi.

So we sit side by side and make a set for me and one for Faiza.

"Minni, do you have any plans for the summer break?" Priya Didi asks.

"Just hanging out with my friend Faiza. And we're joining a volunteer group that's working to clean up the Mithi River and its banks. There's so much plastic and garbage that people thought it'd be impossible to make a dent in it. But the volunteers are doing it."

"Can I join too?" she asks.

"Of course," I say. "It's exciting to see it get cleaner."

"That's terrific, Minni, such a good thing to do," Priya Didi says. "And I was thinking, if you have time, would you like a job here? I'll be teaching all summer and could use help a few days a week. I know you lost your job and could probably use the cash."

Truly speechless, I nod my head again and again, like a bobbing doll. "That would be the best thing ever."

Priya Didi explains more about what the job entails, and when I keep nodding, she grins. "I guess we have a deal."

We go back to our index cards, and it takes me a few minutes to focus. I imagine sharing this news with Sanjay, telling him I can pay for my school fees myself. He must have felt this same kind of pride and satisfaction when he got the job at the restaurant.

After we finish writing all the important dates on cards, Priya Didi quizzes me, and I get almost every answer right.

Priya Didi claps and makes me laugh when she dances around the room. I think back to when Shanti first suggested that we call her didi. Then we did it out of respect. Now I do it because she really *is* like a big sister to me.

Before I leave, Gita comes running back into the classroom. "I had an idea for your app, Minni! Maybe one or two of the neighborhood taps could be labeled as app-taps so it's clear it's the one you reserve online for."

"Great idea. And that's a cool name too," I say.

As I walk home, I feel inspired—and lucky to be surrounded by smart, generous girls.

Lately I've seen way too much of the bad side of human nature. And since I can't "see no evil," I'm happy I can also see the good.

- 45 -

On the day of the exam, I'm strangely numb. I feel like I've been preparing for this forever, and I'm ready to have it be over.

Miss Shah greets me with a squeeze of my shoulder. "You can do this," she whispers.

We wait for the bell that signals the beginning of the exam to ring, and then Miss Shah hands out the exam questions and answer sheet.

I break the seal and start reading.

The first question is *When did India gain freedom from the British?*

1947, I write, picturing the numbers on the cards I made with Priya Didi.

The fan rattles overhead as we work, and finally I am on the last question. When I read it, I smile. It takes me back to my conversation with Shanti. I list the seven lakes that provide water to Mumbai.

I discover that although I might not know every single answer, like I used to when my only responsibilities were to study, tease Sanjay, and run my mouth, I'm positive I know enough to pass—thanks to the people who've helped me, and my own stubborn self.

AFTER THE EXAM, Faiza and I grab each other's hands and run all the way to the top of the hill overlooking the bridge.

Our braids fly, and wisps of hair and the wind tickle our faces as we hug and scream in joy. Something heavy feels like it has dislodged itself from my shoulders.

"Minni," says Faiza, "we did it! Passed our exams and took down a criminal."

"Well, we helped take down a criminal," I say. "Moti mostly did it."

We mime doing karate kicks like crime-fighting Bollywood heroes. "Hi-yah!" we scream as we leap and kick. "Hi-yah!"

The karate chops turn into dance steps, as everything does with Faiza, and we keep at it until we're exhausted and we fall to the ground.

"Doesn't the sea link bridge look like an *M*?" I say. "*M* for Mumbai and *M* for Minni."

"And *M* for May—summer vacation, here we come!" says Faiza. "And don't forget the most important *M*."

"Moti, the wonder dog," we both shout.

Then we sit and stare out at the huge, never-ending Arabian Sea. The view that makes you feel like the world is made of water.

I think of when I was last here with Sanjay. How we spoke about our hopes. And now he is off living his dream. And me, I am working on finding mine. It's hard to believe how much I've grown up since then.

I remember Shanti's words: *Once upon a time, there lived a girl, in our neighborhood, in a city that once was seven islands, who dreamed big dreams and was very lucky.*

Now I really am that girl.

Full of the confidence that everyone has in me and my future. Ready to take on the world and keep dreaming. Like so many who've come before me, I will stay strong, even as the waves crash around me.

Author's Note

MANY OF US don't think about water on a daily basis. We are privileged. But our life and health depend on our ability to obtain water—and a staggering 784 million people worldwide live without basic access to clean water. That's roughly one in ten people on earth.

I was born and raised in Mumbai. A city I love. A city with a major water problem. Like much of India, Mumbai has a fast-growing economy, and while some parts of society are growing richer, a large percentage of the city lives in extreme poverty. Social inequalities continue to rise, and this is most evident in access to education and water. In the 1970s and 1980s, the number of high-rises in the city grew exponentially. Those with resources adapted to the water shortages as best as they could. Storage tanks were built on the rooftops of apartment buildings, and pumps were used to cope with variations in the water supply. But not enough was done to address the lack of water access for the rest of the population—a lack that disproportionally affects the lives of women and children, who generally must spend hours of each day collecting it.

A few years ago, a headline in a Mumbai newspaper about the water mafia grabbed my attention. Water is a big business, and fights over it occur daily. This has led to a black market that can make water access even more unfair. I began to ask questions of Mumbai residents from all walks of life, which led me to a wealth of personal stories that revealed how the struggle for water affected so many parts of people's lives. I hope that Minni's story sheds light on the experiences of many in Mumbai and across the world, and that more support will be given to projects that aim to distribute water more equitably.

World Water Day (March 22) was established by the United Nations in 1993 as an international day to highlight the importance of safe water and bring awareness to the world water crisis.

To learn more about the water situation in India and across the globe, you can visit:

WATER.ORG/OUR-IMPACT/WATER-CRISIS

UN.ORG/EN/GLOBAL-ISSUES/WATER

UNICEF.ORG/INDIA/WHAT-WE-DO/CLEAN-DRINKING-WATER

Acknowledgments

THIRST WAS WRITTEN in 2020, a year of collective trauma, when COVID-19 closed borders, kept me from visiting my family in Mumbai, and bound me to my desk in Houston. The internet allowed me to travel virtually, but when I hit the wall of its limits, my people in Mumbai—Karuna Mangharam and Kalpita Diwan—were generous with WhatsApp calls, pictures, and introductions. My sister, Vrinda Walavalkar, shared articles about the water mafia, and Dr. Nirica Borges answered all my questions about waterborne illnesses.

I owe an immense gratitude to Laxmi Dingankar and Aarti Potdar, both true feminists. During my visit to India in January 2020, over cups of perfect chai and Bollywood music videos, they generously shared life stories that exemplified grit and survival. While neither of them was able to graduate high school, they're determined to make sure their daughters will have that opportunity. Adesh More patiently chaperoned and guided me on my research trips into neighborhoods, and his lived experiences were invaluable.

Caryn Wiseman, my brilliant agent, was a champion of this story from the beginning. Her accepting and flexible style of reading and working makes her a perfect ally. We have many more stories to work on together.

I have the privilege of working with the incredible Nancy Paulsen. She has the superpower of making a manuscript rise above the expectations of its writer. Nancy, thank you for your insightful suggestions and for making me work so hard on Minni's story. Thank you, Sara LaFleur, Cindy Howle, and the entire School and Library team at Penguin Young Readers, who work tirelessly to bring the book into the hands of librarians, teachers, and readers.

Thank you, Anne Bustard, for your steadfast friendship. Christina Soontornvat and Padma Venkatraman, I'm honored by your support; thank you for reading and providing blurbs. Thank you to Sandhya Prabhat for the stunning, evocative cover.

I couldn't do any of this without Rajeev, Samir, and Karishma in my corner. You are my forever home.

WITHDRAWN